# Daisy Lane.

# Daisy Lane.

Stacey Pyne

Daisy Lane
Published by Stacey Pyne
with Castle Publishing
New Zealand
Instagram: goldie_the_book
www.goldiethebook.com

© 2025 Stacey Pyne

ISBN 978-0-473-75557-7 (Softcover)
ISBN 978-0-473-75558-4 (ePUB)
ISBN 978-0-473-75559-1 (Kindle)

Editing:
Iola Goulton

Illustration:
Milla Pyne

Production & Typesetting:
Andrew Killick
Castle Publishing Services
www.castlepublishing.co.nz

Cover Design:
Stephen Kirkby
hi@parkbyprojects.com

Unless otherwise indicated, all Scripture quotations are taken from
the Holy Bible, New Living Translation,
copyright © 1996, 2004, 2015 by Tyndale House Foundation.
Used by permission of Tyndale House Publishers,
a Division of Tyndale House Ministries,
Carol Stream, Illinois 60188.

*For Luke, Livy, Lucy and Jack*

Thank you for your words. I love your stories.


*How sweet your words taste to me;*
*they are sweeter than honey.*
(Psalm 119:103)

# Juniper

Juniper sat on the white marble floor. She crossed her legs beneath her and closed her wings behind her. She opened her right palm. Using the fingers from her left hand, she took some of the manna to her mouth. It was sweet, the bread she loved, and she savoured every bite.

*He rained down manna for them to eat;*
*he gave them bread from heaven.*
*They ate the food of angels!*
(Psalm 78:24–25)

# Rubu

Rubu the bush had always been afraid of fire. Now, here he was, alight with flames and about to burn to death. He couldn't even scream out for help, because Rubu was a bush.

Rubu lived by the mountain of God in Sinai, and God knew everything, so God would already know Rubu was burning. Perhaps it was God's time, because it looked like Rubu would surely shrivel up and die today. Rubu had seen fire and he had witnessed the destruction that it left behind. Rubu would be nothing but a pile of burnt sticks by the day's end.

Rubu didn't want to die. As the flames blazed and crackled all around him, Rubu braced himself for the burn which would inevitably begin any time now. He was surprised to discover the burn seemed to hurt less than he had imagined it might. As the seconds became minutes, Rubu realised the flames did not seem to be hurting him at all, not even a little bit.

There was something else too…

Rubu's branches were not blackening or shrivelling up. They were not burning or falling to the ground. Though the fire kept blazing all around Rubu, his body remained intact. What kind of fire was this?

This was no ordinary blaze. Was God here with Rubu? Could it be that God was rescuing Rubu from the flames this very minute?

There was a sound up ahead, and Rubu realised he wasn't

alone. A man watched Rubu from a distance, and he was clearly as surprised as Rubu by his lack of burning. Why wasn't Rubu burning? The man stepped closer, curiosity written all over his face.

'Do not come any closer.' The voice spoke from the fire, right from where Rubu stood. Rubu felt the voice deep within his branches. It was God's voice. Rubu calmed at the sound of it. Somehow Rubu had wound up here, in the centre of God's story. Although he was on fire, there was nowhere Rubu would rather be.

The man froze, his face full of fear, and Rubu waited and listened.

It was a holy fire. Rubu could feel God now, very close, very still, like a whisper.

'Moses, take off your sandals, for the ground that you are standing is holy,' God told the man. 'I am the God of your father—the God of Abraham, Isaac and Jacob.' Rubu watched as the man flung the sandals from his feet and covered his face with his hands.

There was a long pause. When God again spoke from the fire, Rubu noted the pained tone of his voice.

'I have seen the oppression of my people in Egypt. I have heard their cries for help because of their cruel slave-drivers.'

The man slowly lowered his hands from his face. He didn't come any closer, but he watched Rubu, and he listened to God's voice from the flames, the shock on his face barely subsiding.

'Yes, I am aware of their suffering,' God went on. 'So I have come down to save them from the power of the Egyptians. I will rescue them and lead them out of Egypt into their own spacious and fertile land. It is a land that is flowing with milk and honey.'

The way God spoke of the new land gave Rubu the impression he was fond of it. Rubu wouldn't mind seeing the land for himself.

'Now go, for I am sending you to Pharaoh.'

If the man had looked shocked before, now it looked as though his eyes might pop right out of his head. Rubu wondered if he was afraid.

'You must lead my people out of Egypt,' God commanded him. God had clearly made up his mind. Rubu was sure God knew exactly what he was doing.

*One day Moses was tending the flock of his father-in-law, Jethro, the priest of Midian. He led the flock far into the wilderness and came to Sinai, the mountain of God. There the angel of the Lord appeared to him in a blazing fire from the middle of a bush. Moses stared in amazement. Though the bush was engulfed in flames, it didn't burn up. 'This is amazing,' Moses said to himself. 'Why isn't that bush burning up? I must go see it.'*

*When the Lord saw Moses coming to take a closer look, God called to him from the middle of the bush, 'Moses! Moses!'*

*'Here I am!' Moses replied.*

*'Do not come any closer,' the Lord warned. 'Take off your sandals, for you are standing on holy ground. I am the God of your father—the God of Abraham, the God of Isaac, and the God of Jacob.' When Moses heard this, he covered his face because he was afraid to look at God.* (Exodus 3:1–6)

# A Shift

It looked like an ordinary day in the Kingdom of Heaven. A day filled with love and light and wonder, like it always was here. The sea glistened and the hilltops praised him. Yes, all seemed in order, as it always was. But then something happened.

'Repent of your sins and turn back to our God,' a voice called out in the wilderness. It was the voice of John the Baptist. 'Because the Kingdom of Heaven is near,' John called to the people who were gathered beside the river.

John called out, preparing a way for him. And his voice rang out through the streets of heaven, and his voice was heard by the heavenly beings.

And there was a shift in heaven. And the heavenly beings stood to attention. Because now it was beginning. Because now it had begun.

*And from the time John the Baptist began preaching until now, the Kingdom of Heaven has been forcefully advancing, and violent people are attacking it. For before John came, all the prophets and the law of Moses looked forward to this present time. (Matthew 11:12–13)*

# Daisy Lane

Jovie stood with her feet planted firmly on the pavement and looked down the highway ahead of her. She was trying to decide which way she should go. The highway was broad and had been carefully maintained.

It was clear many had chosen this way before her. The grass was trimmed and impressive flowers lined both sides of the road. There were so many flowers. It seemed no expense had been spared. There were orchids, roses, and tulips of every colour. The colours went on and on for as far as Jovie could see.

But though the wide road was pleasing to the eye and clearly the obvious choice, Jovie had spotted a little lane off to the left of the highway. She turned now, glancing back towards it. The little lane was nothing like the highway. Instead, it was dusty and small, so small she could have missed it if she'd walked by too fast. The little lane was unimpressive, and there were no roses or tulips or manicured gardens. There were only wildflowers. Jovie could only see daisies.

Her gaze wandered back and forth between the highway and the little lane. Back and forth, back and forth. She struggled to put her finger on what it was she was feeling. The wide road was enticing and appeared to be the superior road … so why was there a check in her spirit? Why were the daisies calling to Jovie? The little lane was simple and would likely be harder to navigate. But there was something in her spirit that whispered to her, guiding her back towards it, whispering to her of the daisy lane.

*Enter through the narrow gate. For wide is the gate and broad is the road that leads to destruction, and many enter through it. But small is the gate and narrow the road that leads to life, and only a few ever find it. (Matthew 7:13–14, NIV)*

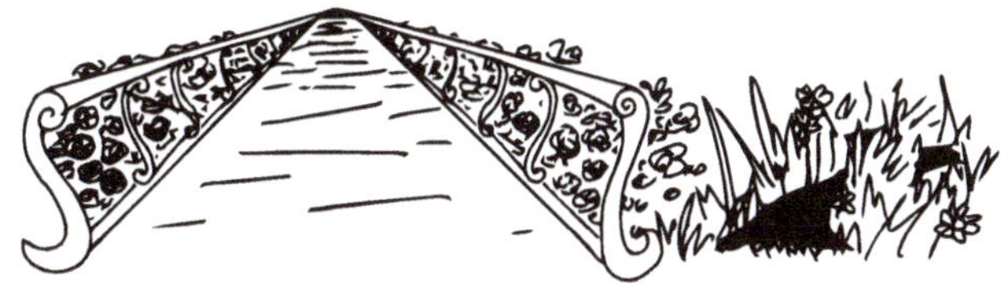

You have kind eyes.


*The Lord is merciful and compassionate,*
*slow to get angry and filled with unfailing love.*
*The Lord is good to everyone.*
*He showers compassion on all his creation.*
(Psalm 145:8-9)

# The Moon

The moon did not speak. He didn't need to. There were no words for him to proclaim. He needn't call out saying, 'I am his witness.'

No.

The moon could just be. It was clear who he was. The way he shone called out for him. The sky that held him whispered silently all around him. The moon had a job to do, and this was it.

*His dynasty will go on forever;*
*his kingdom will endure as the sun.*
*It will be as eternal as the moon,*
*my faithful witness in the sky!*
(Psalm 89:36–37)

# Brilliant Blue

Bezalel sat on the floor, surrounded by folds of linen. It was bright outside, but it was quiet. The people were respectful of Bezalel's work, and they kept their distance during the day.

Bezalel snipped at his final threads and excitement rose within him as he untangled himself from the linen and stood among its folds to shake it out. The colours on this piece were so vibrant. He could already tell it would hold a special place in his heart, perhaps even be among one of his favourite pieces he'd created for the Lord this far.

He held one corner of the linen out in his left hand and stretched his right hand down among the ruffled piles at his feet until he found the other. He shook the curtain out, and it fell in a large flat square, almost covering the entire room. His breath caught in his throat as he took in its beauty.

It was like a dream.

There was something about the blue. Its brilliance was both bold and bright, and stood in perfection beside its purple and scarlet companions, their boldness juxtaposed against the softness of the linen. The curtain was exquisite. Like nothing Bezalel had ever seen, certainly nothing he had created with his own hands.

Bezalel had been given strict instructions, and he knew the colours before him had been chosen by God himself, the fabric, the detailing of the cherubim. Tears pricked at the corners of his eyes at the thought and pride welled up in his spirit. Somehow, Bezalel had been allowed to play a part in his story. The curtain was astounding. It was perfect.

*For the inside of the Tabernacle, Bezalel made a special curtain of finely woven linen. He decorated it with blue, purple, and scarlet thread and with skillfully embroidered cherubim. For the curtain, he made four posts of acacia wood and four gold hooks. He overlaid the posts with gold and set them in four silver bases.* (Exodus 36:35–36)

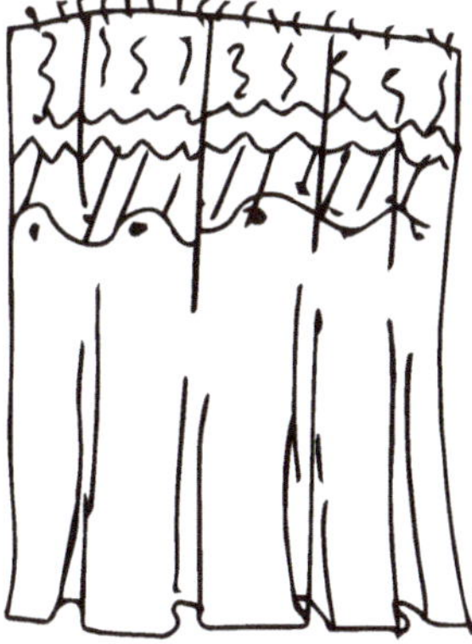

# Joppa

The city of Joppa was perched on a high cliff overlooking the Mediterranean Sea. Its low ledge of rocks hung out over the sea, forming a small harbour below. The sun always shone in Joppa, and the hustle and bustle of the city was exhilarating. Zarel loved living here. She loved everything about Joppa. She loved the brick lanes and the ancient archways that lined the city's roads. She loved the incoming ships arriving at the port every single day, always bringing something new and wonderful. Zarel loved her home.

Today, she stood in the fabric store behind the counter and looked up as a customer stepped inside. It was Tabitha, one of Zarel's regulars. There was something special about Tabitha. She was very kind, but it was more than that ... Zarel had often wondered about her. Tabitha headed straight for the thread section.

'Good morning, Tabitha,' Zarel called out.

'Good morning.' Tabitha replied, but didn't look up. She was clearly on another mission. Zarel left her to browse and returned to her paperwork. She glanced up a few minutes later as Tabitha moved across the floor to the linen wall and again, a few minutes later, as she moved to the centre of the store where the animal skins were stacked up high. Eventually, Tabitha carried her collection to the counter and placed it beside Zarel's pile of papers.

'I'm done, thank you, Zarel.' Tabitha smiled.

Zarel looked over the large pile. She'd been right. Tabitha would be busy today. She nodded, returning Tabitha's smile.

On second glance, Zarel noticed that Tabitha didn't look like her usual self. It was something about her eyes. They were glazed over today, as though Tabitha was tired. Yes, that was it.

Zarel didn't want to intrude or be rude, so didn't say anything. Instead, she got to work, sorting through Tabitha's pile. Zarel added up the total in her mind, but then discounted the price—Tabitha would not be sewing for herself today. She rarely ever was.

After Tabitha had paid, she bundled her collection together under one arm and bid Zarel farewell. Zarel watched as she walked out of her store door. Tabitha stopped on the doorstep and touched her free hand to her head as though nursing a headache.

Had Zarel been right? Was Tabitha feeling unwell today?

But Tabitha only stopped for a brief moment before stepping down into the sunshine. She headed off down the road, towards the sea. Zarel walked around her store, ensuring her fabrics were still neatly folded in their correct piles, before she returned to her paperwork behind the counter.

*There was a believer in Joppa named Tabitha (which in Greek is Dorcas). She was always doing kind things for others and helping the poor. About this time she became ill and died. Her body was washed for burial and laid in an upstairs room. But the believers had heard that Peter was nearby in Lydda, so they sent two men to beg him, 'Please come as soon as possible!'*

*So Peter returned with them; and as soon as he arrived, they took him to the upstairs room. The room was filled with widows who were weeping and showing him the coats and other clothes Dorcas had made for them. But Peter asked them all to leave the room; then he knelt and prayed. Turning to the body he said, 'Get up, Tabitha.' And she opened her eyes!* (Acts 9:36–40)

# Cuba

Cuba the greyhound usually slept through the night, but tonight a sound had woken him. He lifted his head from his bed, and his ears stood up straight on top of his head. Cuba waited and listened.

There it was again.

An odd sound that Cuba had never heard before. It sounded like human voices. Yes, they were human. But they were wailing, far off in the distance. The humans should be asleep at this hour—they always were. What could they be doing?

Cuba should jump up and sound the alarm. He loved to sound the alarm. Cuba had a mighty bark, the loudest in his neighbourhood! But tonight, oddly, Cuba didn't feel like it. He felt tired.

It wasn't like him at all to pass up an opportunity like this. He should get up straight away. He should run outside right now. Instead, he snuggled his head back down into his bed. He shuffled a little, this way and that, before drifting back off to sleep to the sound of wailing voices.

*Then a loud wail will rise throughout the land of Egypt, a wail like no one has heard before or will ever hear again. But among the Israelites it will be so peaceful that not even a dog will bark. (Exodus 11:6–7)*

I find you in places where I am free.

*But whenever someone turns to the Lord, the veil is taken
away. For the Lord is the Spirit, and wherever the Spirit
of the Lord is, there is freedom.* (2 Corinthians 3:16–17)

# Rooney

The doors to his storehouses were thrown open without warning this evening, and Rooney the wind was set free. It was great to be out, and Rooney rushed through the sky, swooping and racing as fast as he could, heading toward the lake. The lake was calm tonight, calm and still … but not for long.

Together with the others, Rooney rushed back and forth over the waters until they came back to life! The waters were wild and alive, sea spray rose high into the sky, and Rooney whooped and hollered, enjoying every moment of it.

It didn't take long. The lake soon looked nothing like it had; all traces of peace had taken off on the wind. Had taken off with Rooney. As the waves rose higher and higher and Rooney howled louder and louder, he noticed a boat. The boat looked very small from Rooney's vantage point, and it was being violently tossed to and fro with the waves that Rooney had stirred up. Rooney was only surprised that the boat was still upright.

He couldn't stop now, though. If the doors to the storehouse remained open, then Rooney had a job to do. And this was it. No, he wouldn't stop.

But then there was a sound. It was a voice. Although it was a whisper, Rooney could still hear it over the howling winds. Could still hear it over his own howling.

'Peace,' the voice whispered. 'Be still.' It was the creator's voice, and his message was clear. But his voice did not come from his storehouse.

No.

His voice came from the little boat that was battling to stay afloat down on the lake.

Rooney didn't know what to think, but he wouldn't wait around to watch. He'd been given instructions, orders by the only one who could control him, so Rooney instantly left. He rushed back towards the storehouse before the doors were once again closed shut behind him.

*Then Jesus got into the boat and started across the lake with his disciples. Suddenly, a fierce storm struck the lake, with waves breaking into the boat. But Jesus was sleeping. The disciples went and woke him up, shouting, 'Lord, save us! We're going to drown!'*

*Jesus responded, 'Why are you afraid? You have so little faith!' Then he got up and rebuked the wind and waves, and suddenly there was a great calm.*

*The disciples were amazed. 'Who is this man?' they asked. 'Even the winds and waves obey him!'* (Matthew 8:23–27)

Lord, thank you that you are close,
even when I'm far away.


*You know when I sit down or stand up.*
*You know my thoughts even when I'm far away.*
*You see me when I travel and when I rest at home.*
*You know everything I do.*
(Psalm 139:2–3)

# Promise

Moses stood before the mountain of God at Sinai. Multitudes of thousands stood behind him. Moses hadn't been sure where to lead them initially, but of course it was here they must go. He stood now, looking up to the mountain—God's Mountain—and in an instant, he was transported back to that day, taken back to the memory.

Moses had been here before.

He had stood here alone.

He had stood in this very spot.

He broke his gaze to glance down to the left of where he stood now and then to the right, scanning the area, searching for the bush where God had met him in the fire.

*I will be with you.*

God's words washed over him now, and he remembered God's promise that day. He spotted the bush. It stood insignificant and unharmed, an ordinary bush.

*And this is your sign that I am the one who has sent you: When you have brought the people out of Egypt, you will worship God at this very mountain.*

And here they were. Moses could hear the laughter of children behind him, the sound of freedom. He fell to his knees in awe of their God, and he raised up his hands in worship.

The people followed behind him, and the sound of many knees dropping to the earth went on and on.

*But Moses protested to God, 'Who am I to appear to Pharaoh? Who am I to lead the people of Israel out of Egypt?'*

*God answered, 'I will be with you. And this is your sign that I am the one who has sent you: When you have brought the people out of Egypt, you will worship God at this very mountain.'* (Exodus 3:11–12)

# Damaris

Damaris wandered down the dusty road. She was late for the council meeting but enjoying the quiet. Instead of speeding up, she slowed down even more and then knelt to the ground in front of an altar. It was the altar to the unknown god. It was small and simple, and Damaris hadn't paid it much attention before.

A candle had been left on the altar but had fallen over and grown dirty. Damaris reached for the candle and used the underside of her robe to clear off the dirt, then placed the candle back in its holder atop the altar.

She cleared away leaves and debris from the little altar, giving it a general tidy-up. When she had finished, she sat back and admired her handiwork. That was much better. She read the inscription again, running the words through her mind.

The unknown god.

It was an intriguing concept. Damaris pondered over it as she continued on with her walk towards the council hall.

Damaris was late by the time she finally arrived, but she had known she would be and didn't mind one bit. As she sat in her seat, joining the others already gathered, she heard the head of the council call a man named Paul to the stand.

Damaris was only half listening as the man began to speak. Instead, she played with a strand of thread that hung from her left sleeve. Why did she feel so restless today? As though there was nowhere she wanted to be and nothing she wanted to be doing.

What was the point of today's meeting anyway? She felt those around her leaning in as Paul spoke, no doubt eager to hear about a new idea. Everybody in Athens loved listening to new ideas. But Damaris was bored.

'I notice you are very religious in every way.' Paul's voice rang out in the auditorium, and Damaris concealed a yawn behind her hand. 'For as I was walking, I saw your many shrines,' Paul went on. 'One of your altars had this inscription on it—"To an unknown god".'

The hairs stood to attention on the back of Damaris's neck, and she sat up in her chair, looking at Paul for the first time since he'd begun to speak. Was it a coincidence that of all the altars in Athens, this man spoke of the altar Damaris had sat before this very morning? She did not know, but she would listen to what Paul had to say.

'This God who you worship without knowing is the God that I am telling you about. He is the God who made our world, and he created everything in it. He is the Lord of both heaven and earth, so he does not live in man-made temples, and human hands cannot serve his needs—for he does not have any needs. He gives life and breath to everything, and he satisfies every single need.'

Damaris was holding her breath and she slowly let it out, though her eyes remained fixed on Paul. What was happening here? Why did it feel like her soul was on fire within her, like it was burning right there in her chest? Burning right through her clothing?

'His purpose was for the nations to seek after him,' Paul continued, 'and perhaps feel their way toward him and to find him—though he is not far away from any one of us. For it is in him that we live and move and exist.'

Damaris had never heard such words spoken of a god before in all her life. And the words seemed to be doing something to her. She could feel the words, as though they were alive. Suddenly, the thread Damaris had been twirling broke free from her sleeve and she watched it as it fell to the ground beside the hem of her robe. Damaris could just make out the soiled patch on the underside of her robe from cleaning the little candle earlier.

The candle on the altar … of the unknown god.

*Then they took him to the high council of the city. 'Come and tell us about this new teaching,' they said. 'You are saying some rather strange things, and we want to know what it's all about.' (It should be explained that all the Athenians as well as the foreigners in Athens seemed to spend all their time discussing the latest ideas.)*

*So Paul, standing before the council, addressed them as follows: 'Men of Athens, I notice that you are very religious in every way, for as I was walking along I saw your many shrines. And one of your altars had this inscription on it: "To an Unknown God." This God, whom you worship without knowing, is the one I'm telling you about.'* (Acts 17:19–23)

You like me.

Regardless of the way I feel.
Regardless of whether I believe it.
Regardless of the things I have done.


*Let me hear of your unfailing love each morning,*
*for I am trusting you.*
*Show me where to walk,*
*for I give myself to you.*
(Psalm 143:8)

# Immie and Elka

Immie and Elka the donkeys had been sent on a strange mission. The donkeys belonged to a wealthy man named Kish who was from the tribe of Benjamin. The donkeys were valuable to Kish and he treated them well, which was why neither of them had ever thought to wander away before.

But that was before God had spoken to them.

It was only a week since God had told them to go for a walk. To go for a long walk far away from their home. Immie and Elka had been confused by his request—they had never left Kish's home alone before.

But, with no more than a worried glance between them, they obeyed God. He was their creator, after all. What else would they do? So they left immediately.

Immie remembered it now, the feeling of stepping out of Kish's gate. The gate had been left open—for them, it seemed. It was never left open, but that day, it was.

So, all on their own, for the very first time, Immie and Elka wandered away. It was the bravest thing they had ever done. Immie had worried about where they would head. He knew Elka would follow him, but how would he lead her? He had never been out alone before.

Immie needn't have worried though, because God had instructed them, of course he did.

*Turn left after this bend, stop here, rest here, turn right now, there is water up ahead.*

His instructions were clear and regular. He was with Immie and Elka, but why? Immie had no idea. As they travelled, Immie and Elka could have sworn they had picked up Saul's scent—Saul was Kish's son.

Had Kish sent Saul to search for his wandering donkeys? They couldn't be sure, but whenever Saul's scent wafted on the air toward them, God would hurry them right along and lead them someplace else.

Finally, after many days of following God's voice, his final instruction had been given to Immie and Elka.

'*Go home,*' he'd told them, so they had. They'd walked safely all the way back to Kish's homestead. They stepped into the gate now, tired from their long walk. Would Kish be pleased to see them?

Their master, Kish, ran out his front door as soon as he heard them approaching. Rather than look to the donkeys or greet them in his excitement, he looked around them and straight through them, his face full of disappointment and concern.

He looked out to the road that lay empty behind them.

*One day Kish's donkeys strayed away, and he told Saul, 'Take a servant with you, and go look for the donkeys.'*

*Now the Lord had told Samuel the previous day, 'About this time tomorrow I will send you a man from the land of Benjamin. Anoint him to be the leader of my people, Israel. He will rescue them from the Philistines, for I have looked down on my people in mercy and have heard their cry...*

*And don't worry about those donkeys that were lost three days ago, for they have been found. And I am here to tell you that you and your family are the focus of all Israel's hopes.'*

*Then Samuel took a flask of olive oil and poured it over Saul's head. He kissed Saul and said, 'I am doing this because the Lord has appointed you to be the ruler over Israel, his special possession. When you leave me today, you will see two men beside Rachel's tomb at Zelzah, on the border of Benjamin. They will tell you that the donkeys have been found and that your father has stopped worrying about them and is now worried about you. He is asking, "Have you seen my son?"'* (1 Samuel 9:3,15-16, 20 & 10:1-2)

Lord, thank you that you care enough to watch my thoughts, and you love me regardless of them.


*For you have seen my troubles,*
*and you care about the anguish of my soul.*
(Psalm 31:7)

# Alex

Alex had lost his appetite recently. In fact, he hadn't been feeling good for some time now. It hadn't even crossed his mind that the last time he felt well was before they had crucified Jesus. No, Alex hadn't paid Jesus another thought since that day.

Until now.

Alex's cousin was the high priest, and he'd called an emergency meeting this morning, inviting Alex along. The meeting was to discuss two of Jesus's disciples, who had recently been thrown into prison. Alex was happy to go along. He had nothing better to do today and nobody to see. Besides, the things he once found pleasure in no longer brought him joy. Even eating had lost its appeal. He pondered his state of mind as the two disciples stood before them in chains.

Alex had lost hope. That was it.

He found himself wondering what the point of anything was. Alex was sad, but he didn't know why. As he watched their faces, it struck him that even the criminals in chains looked happier than Alex felt.

'By what power, or in whose name, have you done this?' the high priest asked the criminals. Alex's attention snapped back to the matter at hand.

The slightly taller criminal stepped forward.

'Rulers and elders.' The criminal's voice was filled with confidence, and Alex sat up in his seat. 'Are we being questioned today because we have done a good deed for a crippled man?'

Alex had heard the story. There was a lame man who was now walking around, but Alex didn't know what had happened.

'Do you want to know how the crippled man was healed?' the criminal asked. 'Let me clearly state to all of you, that he was healed by the powerful name of Jesus the Nazarene, the man you crucified but who God raised from the dead.'

Alex wasn't sure if it was the words that the criminal spoke, or perhaps the way his face seemed to glow as the words fell out of him, but for whatever reason, the blood rushed from Alex's face. If it wasn't for the seat beneath him, he may have fallen over. But what did the disciple mean? Had they healed a lame man using Jesus's name? What did he mean by Jesus was alive again? Alex's head was spinning.

'For Jesus is the one referred to in the Scriptures, where it says, "The Stone that you builders rejected has become the cornerstone." The disciple stepped back again, standing in line with his friend.

The cornerstone, the cornerstone… The words reached Alex somewhere deep inside, touching a place that had been sleeping, a place that had lost hope. There was silence all around Alex, and his world seemed to slow right down. It was a scripture Alex knew well…

What was happening here? Alex didn't understand the disciple's words, but they somehow rang true. A rush of life flooded through his veins for the first time in a long time. Had he missed something? Could he have missed something important? Could he have missed … the cornerstone?

'There is salvation in nobody else! God has given no other name beneath heaven by which we can be saved.' The disciple's voice cracked with emotion. It was clear that the man believed every word that he spoke.

> *The next day the council of all the rulers and elders and teachers of religious law met in Jerusalem. Annas the high priest was there, along with Caiaphas, John, Alexander, and other relatives of the high priest. They brought in the two disciples and demanded, 'By what power, or in whose name, have you done this?' Then Peter, filled with the Holy Spirit, said to them, 'Rulers and elders of our people, are we being questioned today because we've done a good deed for a crippled man? Do you want to know how he was healed?'* (Acts 4:5–9)

# Love Crown

He handed her a crown.
She looked at it, confused. What had she ever done to deserve such a precious gift…
'But why?' she asked him.
'Because you love me,' he replied.

*Afterward they will receive the crown of life that God has promised to those who love him.* (James 1:12)

# Gorgo

Gorgo the demon knew all about Cove's secret. He had used it against her for many years now. Gorgo liked to remind Cove of her secret sin when she was already feeling low, or when she was tired, and especially when she had other problems to deal with.

Gorgo would simply place the memory of her sin inside Cove's mind, then pile it on top of her other worries and watch with glee as he got the better of her all over again. Gorgo was good at what he did. He was one of the best in his master's army… Gorgo thought so, anyway.

As far as Gorgo was concerned, Cove was a sucker. She was easy and weak, and she never put up much of a fight. Gorgo could often have her losing hope again in a matter of minutes. Today would be no different. Gorgo sat close by in Cove's home, watching her in her living room.

Cove sighed and leaned her head back against her sofa. Cove was lonely, and Gorgo was pleased because he hated her. He waited for the perfect time to attack. He assumed tonight would be much like every other night in Cove's boring life. She would drink tea and watch television.

She'd had a bad day at work. Gorgo watched her mind as it relayed the awkward conversation she'd had with her work-mate. Cove always beat herself up about the things she'd said. Gorgo didn't mind—it helped him when Cove got down on herself.

He watched as Cove made herself a hot drink and fetched chocolate from the fridge.

Good. She'd feel guilty about the chocolate in a little while too. He watched and waited for the perfect time. But instead of switching the television on, Cove disappeared upstairs.

Gorgo followed her up and watched as she reached beneath her bed and retrieved her Bible. Gorgo fumed. This was an odd time of the day for her to be reading that. He hated Cove reading it. It was one of the only things Cove did that made his job harder.

But Gorgo wasn't worried though. He had Cove's secret, the secret that cut to her core every time, regardless of whether she read God's word or not. Gorgo followed Cove back downstairs and watched as she read beneath the light of the lamp in the living room. Her tea went cold, and she hadn't even touched the chocolate.

What was going on here?

She seemed to be stuck on one piece of scripture, and Gorgo grew restless watching her. Cove fetched a pen and paper and copied from God's word as she said the words over and over. Gorgo could see she was trying to memorise the words. Gorgo rolled his eyes, though he had grown mildly concerned now.

The timing wasn't perfect, but he'd better use his ammunition now. He was sure he could make Cove put her Bible away and numb her mind with television again instead.

It amazed Gorgo how the humans let their own sin work against themselves. Cove was no different. It never took much effort, either. Just a little reminder here and there, and Cove would run from God all on her own. Run away from him and hide from him.

Thankfully for Gorgo, most humans didn't seem to realise

God was for them and not against them. Gorgo knew this, of course, but he would never reveal it.

Cove turned a page, and Gorgo saw his opportunity as her concentration broke for just a second. He took her sin, her secret sin, and he placed it before her, right in the forefront of her mind. Her addiction clear to see; there was no hiding from it here.

Cove closed her eyes the instant she saw it, and Gorgo smiled. He loved to watch her remember, loved to watch her lose hope again and again and again.

But this time, the memory of Cove's sin seemed to hit up against something.

What was that?

It was something firm, something solid … solid like a wall.

Gorgo's eyes widened, and he realised to his dismay that Cove had discovered the body armour of God's righteousness. Cove had discovered it and now she hid inside it.

Gorgo fumed. He circled the armour, searching for a way in, but it was flawless. There were no cracks. As long as Cove stayed inside, her sin could not reach her. Gorgo knew this—when a human hid inside the armour, God could no longer see their sin. Instead, God saw Jesus, his son, and everyone knew Jesus was flawless.

Gorgo only hoped the body armour was as far as Cove had gotten. Surely she hadn't learned more about God's armour. The armour that was free for all those who belonged to God. It worked in Gorgo's favour that many who did belong to God never even wore it.

Gorgo had plenty of time. He would wait her out. Cove was his priority now. Gorgo would need to break her down today before this got out of hand.

When Cove finally poked her head out, Gorgo was waiting,

and he pounced on her. But his fear was proved right—Cove now wore God's helmet of salvation too. It shone and sparkled, and Gorgo couldn't stand the sight of it. He screamed.

As long as Cove wore the helmet, he couldn't get to her mind. The helmet would ensure she remembered she was saved, regardless of her secret sin. Gorgo stomped around Cove's living room. Perhaps he should call for backup, ask for help, but he couldn't. His pride prevented him. Ever since he'd been assigned to Cove, Gorgo had never had to call for help. And he wasn't going to start today.

This was Cove.

Cove was weak.

Cove was easy.

Gorgo had never had a problem with her before. It wasn't until midnight that Cove rose from the couch and switched off her downstairs light. She carried her Bible up to bed, slid it back under her bed, and climbed beneath the sheets.

Gorgo would have her now. He was sure of it.

He watched her thoughts as she grew sleepy. Just as she drifted off, he aimed and fired her secret sin, always her secret sin.

Cove's eyes flew open, and Gorgo watched in horror as the memory of her sin reverberated off from her and bounced back towards Gorgo. That's when Gorgo realised Cove held the shield of faith.

Cove's sin had hit God's shield.

Cove was holding the shield up for the first time ever, holding it out before her.

As long as Cove held it, she would have faith to believe in God's promises—his promises of forgiveness for her sin, regardless of what it was.

Gorgo's arrows would bounce right off her. Gorgo scowled

at the Bible beneath her bed. It was clear to him now that Cove was no longer just reading the words inside, but she had discovered she could use God's word like a sword.

How had he allowed this to happen right under his nose? He huffed and he puffed, then he screamed out in fury and left Cove's home, both defeated and surprised.

*For we are not fighting against flesh-and-blood enemies, but against evil rulers and authorities of the unseen world, against mighty powers in this dark world, and against evil spirits in the heavenly places.*

*Therefore, put on every piece of God's armour so you will be able to resist the enemy in the time of evil. Then after the battle you will still be standing firm. Stand your ground, putting on the belt of truth and the body armour of God's righteousness. For shoes, put on the peace that comes from the Good News so that you will be fully prepared. In addition to all of these, hold up the shield of faith to stop the fiery arrows of the devil. Put on salvation as your helmet, and take the sword of the Spirit, which is the word of God.* (Ephesians 6:12–17)

I trust you with my body because you made it.

47

*He made their hearts,*
*so he understands everything they do.*
(Psalm 33:15)

# Golden Discovery

Hilkiah loved it here. The temple was his favourite place to be, though he didn't always explore it the way he was exploring today. King Josiah had asked Hilkiah to find and collect all the money that was stored in the Lord's treasury. King Josiah planned to give the money to the supervisors and the workmen. Hilkiah was pleased with Josiah's decision to repair the temple of the Lord his God. The young king showed wisdom far beyond that of his late father. Hilkiah was proud of him, though he didn't speak of it, it was a joy to follow King Josiah's commands.

It was dusty and dim inside the temple today, but always peaceful and deeply sacred. Hilkiah couldn't help but clean some as he sorted through the piles of paperwork and collections. He used an old rag to wipe dust from the surfaces, and he tidied and straightened the scattered scrolls and containers.

As he was dusting a lowered ledge in the back corner of the room, where the minimal lighting made it hard to see at all, he spotted something. A tightly folded scroll, covered in dust, and tucked far back behind the lower ledge. Had it fallen out of sight and been lost? How long had it been down there?

Hilkiah's heartbeat quickened as he reached for the dusty scroll. He felt the Lord's Spirit close beside him, and a tingling sensation that felt like heat ran through his ears and up the back of his neck. He wrapped his fingers around the scroll.

God was here with him now. Hilkiah had the odd feeling that he had stumbled upon something sacred, something of great value. Had this day been planned in advance? Was Hilkiah always supposed to find this scroll? Electricity shot through his body. Was the scroll something important to God? He sensed the answer was yes, based on the thickness of the Spirit's presence. His fingers trembled as he unfolded the delicate paper.

He began to read the written words. What was this? It took him a moment or two to realise the truth.

The scroll had been written by Moses himself.

Hilkiah could not believe his eyes. How had something so precious been misplaced? What were the words written here by Moses that the Israelites were missing out on? No doubt they were important words! Hilkiah moved quickly across the room to where the lighting was better, just slightly better. He sat down, spread the scroll out before him and read it through, every word, from beginning to end.

*While they were bringing out the money collected at the Lord's Temple, Hilkiah the priest found the Book of the Law of the Lord that was written by Moses. Hilkiah said to Shaphan the court secretary, 'I have found the Book of the Law in the Lord's Temple!' Then Hilkiah gave the scroll to Shaphan.*

*Shaphan took the scroll to the king and reported, 'Your officials are doing everything they were assigned to do. The money that was collected at the Temple of the Lord has been turned over to the supervisors and workmen.' Shaphan also told the king, 'Hilkiah the priest has given me a scroll.' So Shaphan read it to the king.*

*When the king heard what was written in the Law, he tore his clothes in despair. Then he gave these orders to Hilkiah, Ahikam son of Shaphan, Acbor son of Micaiah, Shaphan the court secretary, and Asaiah the king's personal adviser: 'Go to the Temple and speak to the Lord for me and for all the remnant of Israel and Judah. Inquire about the words written in the scroll that has been found. For the Lord's great anger has been poured out on us because our ancestors have not obeyed the word of the Lord. We have not been doing everything this scroll says we must do.'* (2 Chronicles 34:14–21)

Even when I sigh, you listen.


*You know what I long for, Lord;*
*you hear my every sigh.*
(Psalm 38:9)

# Eve

Eve looked down at her feet. Her toenails were freshly clipped, but they had still managed to collect dirt beneath them throughout the day. Her feet stood beside her husband's feet. His were much larger in size, and she moved her feet closer to his until her little toe touched the side of his.

Eve and her husband had made a mistake today, and Eve bit her bottom lip as she blinked away her tears. She cowered beside her husband and leaned into him as she grasped his hand inside of her own.

They listened together. They could hear him walking. His was a peaceful pace, his stride always gentle, and his very presence pure joy. He often came in the evening when the cool breezes blew through the garden, and Eve loved it when he came. Eve's heart had always leaped with joy at the sound of his footsteps.

Until today.

Today, for the first time ever, Eve was afraid.

*When the cool evening breezes were blowing, the man and his wife heard the Lord God walking about in the garden. So they hid from the Lord God among the trees. Then the Lord God called to the man, 'Where are you?' (Genesis 3:8–9)*

# The Beautiful Gate

It was about three in the afternoon, and Peter and John were walking into the temple when they saw Tema, the lame man who begged beside the beautiful gate each day. As soon as he saw Tema, Peter knew there was something stirring. The Holy Spirit was near. Peter and John walked by Tema on their way into the temple. Tema held up his hand, hoping for coins. Peter and John exchanged a look before quietly kneeling beside him. They looked at him intently.

'Look at me,' Peter said.

Tema's eyes lit up, and he stretched his hand out towards them.

'I don't have gold or silver to give you,' Peter told him.

Tema looked disappointed and confused, no doubt wondering why they were bothering to talk to him at all.

'But I will give you what I do have.' Peter's palms were burning as he spoke. 'In the name of Christ Jesus, stand up and walk!'

Peter took Tema's right hand in his own and pulled him up from the ground.

'But … I can't.' Tema's protest lasted only a moment, because as his feet stood beside Peter's, they were instantly strengthened and healed. Tema's hand tightened around Peter's as he looked from Peter's eyes down to his feet. Tema released Peter's hand and he leaped into the air. Peter and John laughed, stepping back as Tema jumped around them.

Tears streamed down Tema's face as he praised God. Then he followed Peter into the Temple.

It was only a matter of minutes before the people inside recognised Tema as the lame beggar who lay beside the beautiful gate, day in and day out. The people knew him well, and they were astounded. Peter watched as the crowd turned their attention towards him, thinking Peter had healed Tema using his own power. More and more of the crowd turned their attention towards Peter until Peter realised the opportunity before him. He stepped up on to the base of a column and faced the crowd.

'People of Israel,' he called out. 'Why are you so surprised about this? Why do you stare at us as though we made this man walk by our own power? For it is the God of Abraham, Isaac, and Jacob—the God of our ancestors—who has brought glory to his servant Jesus by doing this. This is the same Jesus who you rejected before Pilate, despite Pilate's decision to release him. You rejected him and demanded the release of a murderer.'

Peter looked out at their faces. They were completely still and completely silent now. Emotion welled up inside him as the words he spoke about Jesus touched his heart.

'You killed the author of life.' He choked on the words, pausing as his words fell over the people. Peter remembered Jesus, his face, his smile, his voice. And Peter remembered that death was no match for him.

'But God has raised him from the dead and he lives.' Peter continued with renewed hope in his voice. 'And we are witnesses of this.' He looked at John, who stood to his left, the bond between them evident. The bond between them Jesus.

*Each day he was put beside the Temple gate, the one called the Beautiful Gate, so he could beg from the people going into the Temple. When he saw Peter and John about to enter, he asked them for some money. Peter and John looked at him intently, and Peter said, 'Look at us!' the lame man looked at them eagerly, expecting some money. But Peter said, 'I don't have any silver or gold for you. But I'll give you what I have. In the name of Jesus Christ the Nazarene, get up and walk!' (Acts 3:2–6)*

# Tulsi

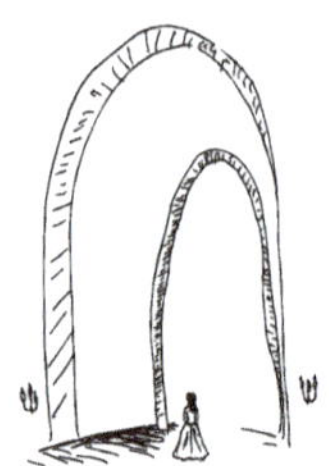

Tulsi had arrived. She was here. It was surreal.

She looked down at the palms of her hands, turning them over and over, back and forth. It didn't feel real. The ceilings were high, so high, the highest ceilings she had ever seen. Tulsi stretched back her neck, taking it all in. She held one hand to her head, securing her crown to be sure it wouldn't fall.

The great hall reminded Tulsi of a ballroom. There was light, so much light. And there was joy—there was no other word for it. Tears quietly dripped from her chin. Tulsi had felt glimpses of this joy throughout her lifetime, but it was no comparison to this. The joy wrapped around her, like liquid love.

She was here.

Tulsi longed to stay here.

She realised her only fear was having to leave. Would it end soon? Would the lights be switched off and the large doors closed for the night? Tulsi wanted to grasp onto this joy she had found, because there was nothing like it.

It was too good. The fall would be too steep.

She longed to stay. Tulsi noticed a line forming beside the large pillars that ran down the right-hand side of the wall. The pillars were huge, white and solid, and there were names all over them.

Pillars. There was something about them. Did Tulsi belong here? Was Tulsi … a pillar? It was an odd thought that came from nowhere … or had it been a whisper?

Tulsi joined the line. Though there were others and Tulsi was not alone, she had eyes only for him. They lined up to see him now, and Tulsi watched him. She had lived a quiet life—she had quietly persevered for him, she had been careful to come to him, to speak with him, to live her life for him. And now here she was.

The line moved slowly, but Tulsi was patient. That had been a hard lesson to learn, but now she was. As she drew nearer, Tulsi watched as the person up front, a woman, stepped toward him. He took what looked like a golden pen and he wrote something on her.

Excitement rose within Tulsi. She longed to be written on by him. What would he write on Tulsi? She had no idea. There was a man who stood in line ahead of Tulsi, and he smiled back at her. Tulsi was worried she might not make it to the front of the line in time.

'Do you know when we will have to leave here?' Tulsi whispered to the man.

'Never,' he replied. The joy in his eyes mirrored her own.

*Because you have obeyed my command to persevere, I will protect you from the great time of testing that will come upon the whole world to test those who belong to this world. I am coming soon. Hold on to what you have, so that no one will take away your crown. All who are victorious will become pillars in the Temple of my God, and they will never have to leave it. And I will write on them the name of my God, and they will be citizens in the city of my God—the new Jerusalem that comes down from heaven from my God. And I will also write on them my new name.* (Revelation 3:10–12)

# Sit Down

He was back beside the Sea of Galilee, a place he loved. He stood on a hilltop and took in the beautiful day. The air was fresh, and the sun shone bright overhead. He breathed deeply, filling his lungs with the fresh sea air.

People had seen him climb the hill. Many were already following, making their way up the hill to be with him. He watched them fondly for a moment before scanning the grassy hilltop around his feet. He would sit down. He chose a spot with thick tufts of grass and sat down, folding his legs beneath him as he waited for the people.

*Jesus returned to the Sea of Galilee and climbed a hill and sat down. A vast crowd brought to him people who were lame, blind, crippled, those who couldn't speak, and many others. They laid them before Jesus and he healed them all.* (Matthew 15:29–30)

Sit down and look fondly at us, Lord. Let us come to you so you can heal us. Do something with us that we could not do ourselves.


*As for me, I look to the Lord for help. I wait confidently for God to save me, and my God will certainly hear me.* (Micah 7:7)

# Minty

Minty was a blackbird who was happy and free. Minty had a home, a nest in a small shrub where he lived with his three young children and their mother, Matilda. Ever since his children had hatched, Minty had fed them. Every day, he would take flight in search of their next meal. Every day, when he found food, he would bring it home to his family. This was the understanding in the blackbird community. Matilda would stay home to protect their young, and Minty would go off and hunt for their next meal.

Today, Minty headed out in search of their next meal. Like every day that had come before this day, Minty didn't worry. Minty didn't have a care in the world when he set off to find food for his family.

It wasn't long before he spotted earthworms down below. It had rained during the night, so worms would be plentiful today. He selected one large earthworm and returned to his nest to deliver it.

Matilda was pleased. She snatched the worm from his beak and fed it to their children.

Minty took off again to find more food. He helped himself to an earthworm before delivering another to their nest. Matilda wanted berries. She loved berries, and Minty knew exactly where to find them.

On his way to the foliage, he spotted a snail beneath a tree amongst the leaves. Yum! Minty flew back to the nest with the snail and delivered it to Matilda to feed to their children.

Now he would collect some berries. The foliage was close to their home, so he went back and forth, carrying as many berries as he could until he had delivered more than enough.

No, Minty never worried about finding food or about going hungry, because he trusted his heavenly Father. Minty's heavenly Father had fed them every single day of Minty's life. Being a father himself, Minty understood this. Minty would never stop feeding his own children, and his heavenly Father would never stop feeding them.

*That is why I tell you not to worry about everyday life— whether you have enough food and drink, or enough clothes to wear. Isn't life more than food, and your body more than clothing? Look at the birds. They don't plant or harvest or store food in barns, for your heavenly Father feeds them. And aren't you far more valuable to him than they are? Can all your worries add a single moment to your life?* (Matthew 6:25–27)

Remind me how to find you
when my world feels dark.
When I am so far from you.
When I have forgotten.


*Turn to me and have mercy,*
*for I am alone and in deep distress.*
*Feel my pain and see my trouble.*
*Forgive all my sins.*
*May integrity and honesty protect me,*
*for I put my hope in you.*
(Psalm 25:16,18,21)

# Ghost

Peter had been alive for twenty-eight years, and he had never seen a ghost. He had heard scary stories and rumours about ghosts, but he had never believed them. But today, out in the middle of the lake, in the middle of a storm, he saw one.

The ghost was a man, dressed in white, and he shone, hovering above the water. Or was he walking on the water? Peter couldn't tell, but the ghost was headed toward their boat. Peter was awestruck.

'It's a ghost,' Peter cried out. He squinted, wiping the seawater from his eyes, trying to see clearer.

'Get away from it,' Luke yelled over the raging waters. His voice was panicked, and clearly Peter wasn't the only person who was seeing things. The others could see the ghost too. The disciples, who were already battling the waves, now desperately tried to paddle away from the shining man.

'Do not fear,' the ghost called out to them. It was a familiar voice, a voice which Peter recognised straight away.

Jesus.

'Have courage, do not be afraid. I am right here,' the ghost told them. Though he wasn't close, they could still hear his voice. Could it really be Jesus?

'Lord, is it really you? Let me come to you walking on the water,' Peter called back. He regretted his words as soon as they were out.

'Yes, come to me,' the ghost replied.

Peter gripped the side of the boat with both hands and looked at the surface of the water. It was wild, uneven, and choppy. But all eyes were on him now. Peter held on tight to the boat's side as he lifted one foot overboard, then the other.

His feet didn't sink.

He let go of the boat one hand at a time. Matthew whooped in amazement, and the rest of the disciples were silent as they watched in wonder. Peter stood, staring at his floating feet, before he turned around to face Jesus and took a step toward him.

Peter could see him now. It was his face, the face of Jesus on the ghost. A face Peter loved. A wave came up behind him. Peter broke eye contact with Jesus as he realised the wave was going to hit him.

What on earth was he doing out here? How would he survive this? This couldn't end well. That's when Peter realised he was now thigh-deep in the water. He was sinking.

'Lord, help me,' he shouted, panic rising with each second.

Jesus was beside him in an instant, his hand wrapped around Peter's arm. Jesus pulled Peter from the water and his feet once again rested on the surface.

'Why didn't you trust me?' Jesus asked him. 'You have so little faith.'

They climbed back into the boat. The wind and waves stopped, and the sky quieted. The wild storm coming to a complete stand still in mere moments.

Jesus sat on the side of the boat, his clothing dripping all over the deck, and Peter fell to his feet before him. He knelt so low that his nose touched the deck, and his tears mingled with the lake water puddling there.

The disciples were silent, in awe of Jesus. They bowed their heads before him one by one. There was a deep calm on board the boat now. The realisation settling over all aboard… he really was the Son of God.

> *When they climbed back into the boat, the wind stopped. Then the disciples worshipped him. 'You really are the Son of God!' they exclaimed.* (Matthew 14:32–33)

# Sully

Sully sat with her Mama on the mat beside the door. The door was open, and the curtain blew in the evening breeze. It was still light outside though, and Sully watched the road as a group of children walked past their home. Sully's Mama was mending a cloak beside her. Sully wanted to run back out to play, but she was hungry. Her stomach grumbled.

'Is dinner almost ready?' Sully asked her Mama. Mama placed the cloak down and jumped up to check on their dinner. She was back in a couple of minutes with bread that smelled delicious. She handed Sully the bread and sat back down to resume her mending.

Sully looked from Mama to the bread in her hand. The bread was flat, nothing like the bread Sully was used to. Sully opened her mouth to protest. Without even looking up, Mama answered her question before she'd asked it.

'It is Passover, Sully, so we must eat our bread without yeast now.'

Sully vaguely remembered eating the flat bread once before, but she was only five years old now. She couldn't remember further.

'How long will we eat flat bread?' she asked. Mama turned the cloak over, inspecting it in her hand.

'For seven days,' Mama replied.

Sully was suspicious of the bread. As hungry as she felt,

she still didn't take a bite. She thought about it for a minute or so, eyeballing the funny-looking bread.

'But why?' she asked Mama.

Mama placed her cloak down again and turned to face Sully. She smiled down at her and moved the hair back from Sully's forehead.

'Because, Sully, many years ago, before you were born, on this very day, God rescued us from slavery in Egypt.' Sully had heard the stories before, but she liked to hear them, so she remained still and quiet and listened to Mama.

'God rescued us in the middle of the night. God's angel of death struck every house in Egypt, but he passed over our homes. This is why we call it the Passover. We were in such a rush to leave Egypt that night that we did not have time for our bread to rise.' Sully looked back to the bread in her hand and flopped it back and forth as she thought of the Israelite children who would have eaten it on the night of their escape.

'We remember how he rescued us every year now, at this time, by eating our bread without yeast, like that night,' Mama said.

Sully stared at her Mama with wide open eyes, then she nodded and took a big bite out of her flat bread. Mama laughed at Sully and tussled her hair.

'How does it taste?' Mama asked.

'It tastes good,' Sully replied.

*For seven days the bread you eat must be made without
yeast. Then on the seventh day, celebrate a feast to the Lord.
On the seventh day you must explain to your children,
'I am celebrating what the Lord did for me when I left*

Egypt.' This annual festival will be a visible sign to you, like a mark branded on your hand or your forehead.

And in the future, your children will ask you, 'What does all this mean?' Then you will tell them, 'With the power of his mighty hand, the Lord brought us out of Egypt, the place of our slavery.' (Exodus 13:6,8–9,14)

# His Home

He was dressed in a magnificent robe made of light. It hung from his shoulders and dropped all the way to the floor, sending shimmers of light wherever he moved.

Evening approached, so he pulled his curtains closed. His curtains shone and they twinkled because they were the stars of the heavens. His curtains were the night sky.

He sat in his living room and rested his head back to look up at the rafters of his home. They were the rain clouds. The rafters of his home were the clouds that brought the rains.

He moved to his bathroom, where he turned on the faucet. The water that ran from it rained down on to the mountains, he watered the mountains from his heavenly home. He was intertwined with it all, his home supplying the needs of our home, each and every detail.

*You are dressed in a robe of light. You stretch out the starry curtain of the heavens; you lay out the rafters of your home in the rain clouds. You send rain on the mountains from your heavenly home, and you fill the earth with the fruit of your labour. (Psalm 104:2–3,13)*

# Light

She was surrounded by darkness, and he wanted her to see. So he took a lamp and created a flame. He touched the flame to the wick, and the wick came alive with light. He then placed the chimney over the lamp's base.

Lifting the lamp in one hand, he stepped into her darkness. He did not hesitate because her darkness did not scare him. He stood right beside her now.

Though she could not see him and though her eyes remained closed, she was instantly surrounded by his brilliant light. It reached inside her, all the way to her core. He had stepped into her darkness again, rescued her like only he could, lit a light so she would be able to see.

*You light a lamp for me.*
*The Lord, my God, lights up my darkness.*
(Psalm 18:28)

# Teddy

Teddy had collected pearls for many years, and his collection was more valuable to him than anything else in his life. Over the years, Teddy had risked his life many times in pursuit of his pearls. Now he was older and his hunting days were over, he inspected his pearl collection every single day. Teddy would admire his pearls, and he would clean his pearls, and sometimes, when he was all alone, he would even speak to his pearls.

It was true. Teddy's pearl collection came second to nothing in Teddy's life.

Today, Teddy sat in his favourite chair beside the fireplace and opened his pearl case. He ran his eyes over each one before selecting the largest of his pink pearls. He leaned back in his chair and held the pearl up before his eyes. He slowly turned the pearl between his thumb and forefinger. It was exquisite. After all these years, her raw beauty still took his breath away. He remembered the day he'd discovered her as if it was yesterday. He remembered the rope was tied to his waist and the large rock that weighed him down beneath the water. It had been a dangerous mission. He had risked his life for her, and for many of his pearls. Yes, there was a story behind each one.

Teddy had become a wealthy man because of his pearl collection, and he was always on the lookout for new pearls to add to it, though his searching looked a little different nowadays.

There was a pearl merchant visiting Teddy's hometown today, so he would head into town to see what the merchant had to offer. He rarely came across a pearl that compared to those in his own collection. Teddy's pearls were a great treasure, a lifetime's work, his greatest achievement.

Teddy carefully stored his pearls back in their case, then readied himself to go into town. He decided to take his case with him. He doubted he would need it, but he always felt better when his pearls were near.

Teddy had low expectations when he arrived at the home where the merchant was staying.

A woman met him at the door.

'Can I help you?' She asked.

'Yes,' Teddy replied. 'I am here to see the pearl merchant who is visiting.'

The woman led Teddy into a kitchen. It was run down, and natural sunlight poured in through a hole in the ceiling. But Teddy had already spotted the pearls spread out on the countertop, displayed for visitors to browse over.

'Keeka will be in shortly,' the woman told Teddy as she turned to leave.

But Teddy did not reply, because a pearl had caught his eye. It was a golden pearl.

Teddy squinted unbelieving eyes. He had never seen a golden pearl before. He hurried across the room. He kneeled down until his face was counter height and inspected the unusual pearl. He was right. It was golden. He let out the breath he'd been holding. His hands felt clammy. Teddy pulled at the neck of his garment. Had it become hot in here all of a sudden?

He was sure of one thing. The golden pearl was the most beautiful thing Teddy had ever seen. His vision blurred and the golden pearl became hazy, but he had to touch it. He had to touch it. More than that, he had to own it. He gently took thumb to forefinger around the golden pearl and lifted it from the counter. He lifted it up, into the light. There was a shuffle behind him.

'I see you've found goldie.' Keeka stood behind him.

Teddy was speechless. He turned, looking from the golden pearl into Keeka's eyes, and then straight back up to the pearl.

'I'll take it,' Teddy said. He would do anything to take the golden pearl with him today. He couldn't leave without it. Keeka chuckled and shook his head, just slightly.

'I don't think so,' Keeka replied. 'It is worth a great deal. I would not part with her for any less than her full worth … and some.'

Teddy placed the golden pearl back on the counter, silent. He remained calm, though panic rose within him because he must own the golden pearl. There was nothing he desired more.

Teddy carefully lifted his case onto the tabletop. He opened it up, his beautiful collection, and motioned for Keeka to look at the display. Keeka let out a slow whistle as he looked over Teddy's collection.

'Impressive,' he finally said.

Teddy nodded. The two men locked eyes, and the silence stretched between them.

'I'll take your whole collection in exchange for the golden pearl,' Keeka finally offered.

'It's a deal,' Teddy replied. There was no hesitation.

'I will take your home, too, and all your belongings,' Keeka added.

'Yes,' Teddy replied. 'They are all yours.'

Teddy had just exchanged everything he owned, but his

gaze had already wandered back to the golden pearl. Now, Teddy owned nothing except for the pearl. But he had no regrets, because there was nothing worth more than the golden pearl.

74

> *Again, the Kingdom of Heaven is like a merchant on the lookout for choice pearls. When he discovered a pearl of great value, he sold everything he owned and bought it!* (Matthew 13:45–46)

I will always say yes to your body.
I will always say yes to who you are.


*As they were eating, Jesus took some bread and blessed it. Then he broke it in pieces and gave it to the disciples, saying, 'Take it, for this is my body.'*

*And he took a cup of wine and gave thanks to God for it. He gave it to them, and they all drank from it. And he said to them, 'This is my blood, which confirms the covenant between God and his people. It is poured out as a sacrifice for many.'* (Matthew 14:22–24)

# Bell

Bell wasn't convinced. She didn't say so, but her expression no doubt gave her away. Moses and Aaron stood before them with a far-fetched story about how God had spoken to them. About how God wanted to rescue Bell and her people from their slavery in Egypt.

Just that morning, Bell had listened from behind a closed door as her husband was beaten by an Egyptian slave driver. Bell knew better than to cry out or to try to help him—she had made that mistake before. Instead, she had listened helplessly as they all but bashed the life out of Lemo.

Lemo was strong. He could have fought back.

But then he would have been killed. It was humiliating for Lemo, and Bell felt his humiliation as though it were her own. Silent tears had dripped down her face as she leaned her head against her crossed arms.

*Please help us.*

They were the only words she had muttered, mouthing them silently to the only one who had the power to help them. She had often asked him … but he had never listened.

She squinted now, hardening her expression as Moses and Aaron went on and on. They were certainly animated in their storytelling. But why?

Bell wouldn't let herself believe that God had actually heard their cry, that he had remembered them in their slavery.

'Yahweh, the God of Abraham, Isaac and Jacob has spoken

to me.' Moses pleaded with the crowd again, his arms stretched out wide. 'God says, "I have been watching closely, and I have seen how the Egyptians are treating you. I have promised to rescue you from your oppression in Egypt. I will save you and lead you to a new land. A land that is flowing with milk and honey".'

Bell didn't want the words to penetrate through her tough exterior, but she felt them somewhere deep down within. Yet she was careful not to reveal a change in her expression.

Bell watched as old man Eber dropped down to his knees before Moses and Aaron. He leaned all the way forward until his head touched the ground. Then he called out, worshipping God.

Bell was surprised. Eber was a wise man. Did he believe what Moses and Aaron were proclaiming? That God was going to rescue the Israelites?

Others followed Eber's lead and fell to their knees in worship. Bell looked to Lemo. Lemo's left eye was bruised and blackened. His eyes could barely open after the beating, but there was no mistaking that they were moist. Lemo believed Moses and Aaron too. He dropped to his knees beside Bell to worship.

*Then the people of Israel were convinced that the Lord had sent Moses and Aaron. When they heard that the Lord was concerned about them and had seen their misery, they bowed down and worshipped. (Exodus 4:13)*

# The Crystal Sea

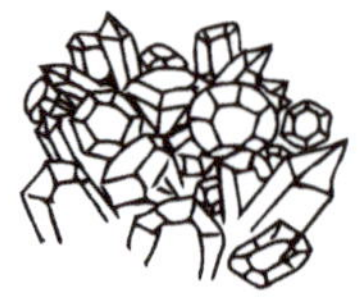

Every time John tried to pen it, he was overcome with emotion, as though the Spirit within him carried him straight back to that place. Thankfulness flooded his being until once again he held his head in his hands and wept. It was all he could do.

The memories overwhelmed him in the best possible way. He'd been transported by the Spirit that day, through time and space and into the very throne room of heaven.

How had he survived? How had he lived to tell of the day?

John knew it was for this reason that he had lived—that he must tell of the day. But words escaped him. It was too much. He picked up his pen and took it to his paper. He would try again.

He closed his eyes and saw their crowns. They surrounded his throne, elders all dressed in white. John remembered his throne. It had been hard to look at, because of the blinding light that surrounded, emanating from him, pouring out in every direction from where he sat.

There had been sound too, great booms of thunder and flashes of lightning had rung out from his throne, and the glow of an emerald rainbow surrounded him. But it was the shiny sea of glass that sparkled like crystal before the throne that John remembered today.

He held his palms to his eyes, recalling the glass sea and how he had felt looking into its depths and what he had seen inside of it. He opened his eyes and felt the Spirit near as he wrote of the sea.

It had been real.

John had stood before his throne. Now, he felt the Spirit guiding his fingers as the words poured out of him, and he smiled to himself. Only with the Spirit's help would he ever be able to describe it.

*Then as I looked, I saw a door standing open in heaven, and the same voice I had heard before spoke to me like a trumpet blast. The voice said, 'Come up here, and I will show you what must happen after this.' And instantly I was in the Spirit, and I saw a throne in heaven and someone sitting on it. The one sitting on the throne was as brilliant as gemstones—like jasper and carnelian. And the glow of an emerald circled his throne like a rainbow. Twenty-four thrones surrounded him, and twenty-four elders sat on them. They were all clothed in white and had gold crowns on their heads. From the throne came flashes of lightning and the rumble of thunder. And in front of the throne were seven torches with burning flames. This is the sevenfold Spirit of God. In front of the throne was a shiny sea of glass, sparkling like crystal.* (Revelation 4:1–6)

Let my life speak of your life.

*But blessed are those who trust in the Lord and have made the Lord their hope and confidence. They are like trees planted along a riverbank, with roots that reach deep into the water. Such trees are not bothered by the heat or worried by long months of drought. Their leaves stay green, and they never stop producing fruit.* (Jeremiah 17:7–8)

# Layla

Layla had a golden necklace she had always treasured. It was rare and flawless and simply exquisite. The necklace had belonged to Layla's grandmother, and Layla knew nobody else who owned such a beautiful piece. This was why Layla now stood at her front door, her mouth agape, as she watched an Israelite slave walk away with her treasured necklace.

Layla would have run after her to demand the return of her necklace … except Layla had given it to her. Layla had gifted her most prized possession to an Israelite slave she didn't even know. An Israelite slave who had knocked on Layla's door and asked Layla for her golden necklace. The surprise in her eyes matched Layla's as she handed the necklace over, placing it in the hands of a stranger.

Now she was left with only a question: what on earth had come over her?

*And the people of Israel did as Moses had instructed; they asked the Egyptians for clothing and articles of silver and gold. The Lord caused the Egyptians to look favorably on the Israelites, and they gave the Israelites whatever they asked for. So they stripped the Egyptians of their wealth!* (Exodus 12:35–36)

Your words taste better than life.

82

*They are more desirable than gold,*
*even the finest gold.*
*They are sweeter than honey,*
*even honey dripping from the comb.*
(Psalm 19:10)

# Night Mission

It was eerie and still being in the city of Jerusalem so late in the night. But even though a blanket of darkness lay over the city, Nehemiah could still make out the destruction all around him. Jerusalem. Their beautiful city. His heart wept for the city, for their home.

He had slipped out in secret and entered through the Valley Gate tonight, passing by the Jackal's Well. He now sat atop his donkey, beside the Dung Gate. The walls of Jerusalem lay in ruins, torn down for as far as Nehemiah could see, and the city's gates had been all but burned to the ground. Nehemiah had heard the reports about the city, but this was worse than he had imagined. How had this happened to Jerusalem? To the place their God had chosen for his name to be honoured?

The only sound against the stillness of the night was Nehemiah's breath. His donkey sat still beneath him.

As Nehemiah looked at the destruction before him, it was hard not to feel defeated. He had been filled with blind hope until now, but now that he saw the destruction, the prospect of restoring their city was overwhelming. Where would he even begin?

Nehemiah instructed his donkey to turn around on the spot, the rubble moving beneath his feet as he slowly turned, a stark contrast to the quiet of the night. The city had been ruined, completely abused by their enemies.

Yet although destruction was all he could see with his

human eyes, something deep inside of Nehemiah remained unmoved, and he could not shake the feeling that God was with him, that God was helping him. Hadn't God placed this task in his heart to begin with? Or had the desire to bring the city of Jerusalem back to life been Nehemiah's idea alone? No, God was with him.

Nehemiah remembered last week's conversation with the king! The conversation could have gone either way, and he remembered the fear he had felt and the words he had whispered in prayer to God.

*Put it into his heart to be kind to me*, Nehemiah had prayed. *Please give me favour with the king, let me succeed today.*

God had heard Nehemiah's desperate plea and had caused the king not only to allow Nehemiah to return to Jerusalem, but he had sent with him letters of recommendation too. The king had even supplied wood to begin the rebuild.

Nehemiah continued on now, as quietly as possible, leading his donkey up to the Fountain Gate and the King's Pool. It was nostalgic. It had been so very long since he was last here, and the memories came flooding back to him. They were memories of a happier time, where laughter rang through the streets, where there was dancing and a sense of security.

The rubble became too thick, and his donkey struggled to step through it, so Nehemiah gave up and changed direction. He paused, eyeing the Kidron Valley. It was too dark to go that way, but Nehemiah was desperate to see and inspect that wall as well. They would take it slowly.

His donkey stepped cautiously up through the Kidron Valley. The further Nehemiah went, the clearer the extent of the destruction became. But so did his resolve to trust in the one he could not see. When Nehemiah left the city back out through the Valley Gate, he had made up his mind. He would do whatever it took. He would work as hard as he ever had, to restore their city, Jerusalem.

*So I arrived in Jerusalem. Three days later, I slipped out during the night, taking only a few others with me. I had not told anyone about the plans God had put in my heart for Jerusalem. We took no pack animals with us except the donkey I was riding. After dark I went out through the Valley Gate, past the Jackal's Well, and over to the Dung Gate to inspect the broken walls and burned gates. Then I went to the Fountain Gate and to the King's Pool, but my donkey couldn't get through the rubble. So, though it was still dark, I went up the Kidron Valley instead, inspecting the wall before I turned back and entered again at the Valley Gate.* (Nehemiah 2:11–15)

I am so thankful that I know where my life ends.
That it begins and ends with you.


*'I am the Alpha and the Omega—the beginning and the end,' says the Lord God. 'I am the one who is, who always was, and who is still to come—the Almighty One.'*
(Revelation 1:8)

# Lion

Lion shook his great mane, and the six wings on his back shook with him, following along after his great frame. The eyes that covered his wings did not close with the movement, not even to blink. The eyes on Lion's wings remained open always. Lion could see, in every direction, at all times. And because of this, Lion had great understanding. In fact, Lion understood everything.

Lion looked to his right, into Eagle's many eyes, and then to his left, to Ox and to Human. Lion nodded at his companions. No words were needed. They all knew what to do. Lion opened his mouth. In unison, they poured out the truth.

'Holy, holy, holy is the Lord God, the Almighty,' they shouted, 'the one who always was, who is, and who is still to come.' Their voices wove together, creating a mighty roar of power and life. Lion would never stop declaring it. He would never cease to call out his name.

*In the centre and around the throne were four living beings, each covered with eyes, front and back. The first of these living beings was like a lion; the second was like an ox; the third had a human face; and the fourth was like an eagle in flight. Each of these living beings had six wings, and their wings were covered all over with eyes, inside and out. Day after day and night after night they keep on*

saying, 'Holy, holy, holy is the Lord God, the Almighty—
the one who always was, who is, and who is still to come.'
(Revelation 4:6–8)

# Rosa

Rosa huddled in the corner of the square. She tried to hide behind the others, but they were trying to hide themselves. So Rosa stopped, arms by her side, and she looked to Jesus. It was all she could do.

Rosa knew it was him and she calmed at the sight of him. Rosa had always known him, though this was the first time her eyes had known him.

Jesus saw Rosa too. His gaze moved from Rosa to the others beside her and he smiled. He pointed to them.

'They are mine,' he announced to his Father and the angels. He sounded sure.

*They will walk with me in white, for they are worthy. All who are victorious will be clothed in white. I will never erase their names from the Book of Life, but I will announce before my Father and the angels that they are mine.* (Revelation 3:4–5)

# Tove

Tove sold doves for a living, and today would no doubt be another big business day in the temple. He was very particular about setting up his stall table. He liked to ensure he had plenty of time to get it right. Tove's table was a simple design compared to some of the others, but Tove had constructed his table himself and he was proud of it.

Tove started with the three table legs. They were heavy and sat low to the ground. The temple floor had been swept clean in preparation for another market day, so the legs sat flat and moved easily across the floor.

Next, Tove steadied his tabletop securely on the table legs, then stacked the dove cages one on top of another. He had many shapes and sizes, and displaying them all was a bit like placing the pieces of a jigsaw puzzle together. But Tove had many days of practice beneath his belt, and the doves were displayed to perfection in no time.

He stood back to take in his handiwork. His stall was almost complete.

Tove sorted through the coins in his money tin at his feet beneath the table. He might need more change to see out the full day, but he would just have to wait and see. Last of all, Tove set up his chair behind his stall table. It was a simple chair, but it did the trick. After all, Tove would be working for many hours now. He would need to rest between customers in order to see out the entire day.

Before he knew it, the large doors were opened to the public, and streams of people flooded in. Tove had been right—it would be another busy market day in the temple.

Tove got to work straight away, serving one customer after another as they passed by his stall. He was just finalising his third dove sale for the morning when there was an almighty crash at the stall next door. Coins exploded to the floor and rolled away in every direction. Not only that, but the entire tabletop seemed to have fallen.

A coin darted beneath Tove's legs, and he crouched to retrieve it. It was as Tove was crouching behind his stall table with the coin between his fingers that the empty chair beside him was lifted into the air and thrown to the ground. The loud crash of Tove's chair echoed up the temple walls.

Tove jumped back and cowered beneath his table, as he glimpsed the face of the man who had thrown it. Tove did not recognise his face. The man moved from Tove's stall to Tove's neighbours, where he grabbed hold of their chair and lifted it above his head. The chair came crashing down, hitting Tove's chair and then lying still beside it.

What was going on here? Who was this man? Why was he causing such a scene and destroying their market stalls? Tove would have protested, but the fury in the stranger's eyes stopped him from moving. Instead, he froze in his hiding place beneath his stall and watched as the stranger went from one stall to the next, destroying every single one.

*Jesus entered the Temple and began to drive out all the people buying and selling animals for sacrifice. He knocked over the tables of the money changers and the chairs of those selling doves. He said to them, 'The Scriptures declare,*

*"My Temple will be called a house of prayer," but you have turned it into a den of thieves!'* (Matthew 21:12–13)

*Then his disciples remembered this prophecy from the Scriptures: 'Passion for God's house will consume me.'* (John 2:17)

Let me believe that you love me, Lord.


*Jesus told them, 'This is the only work God wants from you: Believe in the one he has sent.'* (John 6:29)

# Runaway Heart

Beth had slept with her daughter all night. She hadn't meant to, but had lain beside Rebekah, stroking her forehead, until she slept. Then Beth had watched Rebekah, thanking God for her with all of her heart. Somewhere, amidst her prayers deep into the night, sleep had found her, too.

Now Beth was pleased she'd slept beside her daughter, that she'd watched her breathing, that she'd studied her sleeping features. Beth listened to the conversation unfold between Laban and Abraham's servant, and the lump grew inside of her throat and the realisation settled around her.

Rebekah would leave today.

This very day.

Beth knew the likelihood of ever seeing her daughter again was slim, and fresh tears sprang to her eyes at the thought. Beth had presumed they would have time. They'd heard only yesterday that Rebekah would leave home, and Beth had imagined they would have at least a week to get used to the idea.

How would Beth let her daughter leave so soon? Rebekah was her girl—her best friend, her own heart walking around outside of her body.

They called for Rebekah now and Beth hardly spoke a word. Instead, she held her breath and listened.

'Will you go with this man?' Laban was asking.

Rebekah looked to Beth then. Her baby. Her wide eyes said it all. Beth had watched the same expression on her daughter's face countless times before. Rebekah wanted Beth's help. She needed her mother's opinion. It was a huge decision, the biggest that Rebekah had ever been faced with.

Beth fought back her tears. Using all the strength she could muster, she smiled at her daughter. They had never been apart before, and though this was the hardest thing Beth had ever been asked to do by their God, she knew it was he who asked. She knew he was trustworthy.

'I will go with him,' Rebekah replied. Pride welled within Beth's chest at the strength in her daughter's voice. Then Beth looked to Debby. Debby had been Rebekah's childhood nurse and had always been with her. Beth and Debby spoke to one another without any words.

Debby loved Rebekah. Debby would go with Rebekah. Debby would be with her when Beth could not.

The thought brought Beth immense comfort. One thing was clear. God had a plan for her daughter's life.

*'But we want Rebekah to stay with us at least ten days,' her brother and mother said. 'Then she can go.'*

*But he said, 'Don't delay me. The Lord has made my mission successful; now send me back so I can return to my master.'*

*'Well,' they said, 'we'll call Rebekah and ask her what she thinks.' So they called Rebekah. 'Are you willing to go with this man?' they asked her.*

*And she replied, 'Yes, I will go.'*

*So they said goodbye to Rebekah and sent her away with Abraham's servant and his men. The woman who had been Rebekah's childhood nurse went along with her.*
(Genesis 24:55–59)

# Power Nap

John sat beside Jesus, listening. He kept his eyes low and watched the hairs on Jesus's arm beside him. John was tired and didn't want to get involved in the conversation. So his head remained low, and he watched as the hairs on Jesus's forearm moved ever so slightly with the wind. John knew his arms well ... almost as well as if they were his own.

John adored Jesus. He had never studied anyone so closely. Jesus had a small scar close to his left wrist, and a trail of light moles wove up his forearms. The skin of his arms was darkened from the sun, and a light covering of hair protected them.

John was tired. He could tell this conversation was still far from over, but he needed a rest. He waited for a pause in the discussion, then reached out his hand and touched Jesus's arm to excuse himself. He would find somewhere to take a quick nap.

*We proclaim to you the one who existed from the beginning, whom we have heard and seen. We saw him with our own eyes and touched him with our own hands. He is the Word of life. This one who is life itself was revealed to us, and we have seen him. (1 John 1:1–2)*

# Tink's Hidden Treasure

Tink the worm had made an interesting discovery today. He was busy squirming beneath the great tree near Shechem when he found it. The dirt seemed to come to an abrupt halt, and Tink almost smacked his head right into the shiny object before him.

It was a deep pit, well hidden beneath the great tree near Shechem. A pit that seemed to be filled to the brim with precious jewels. There were earrings and pagan idols made from silver, gold, and precious stones. The treasures had been left in the pit, then covered with fresh dirt for the likes of Tink to discover. The earrings no longer shone or twinkled in the sunlight. Instead, they lay in the dirt with Tink, their shimmer dulled, and their beauty hidden from the world.

They lay in the dirt now, where they belonged.

*So Jacob told everyone in his household, 'Get rid of all your pagan idols, purify yourselves, and put on clean clothing. We are now going to Bethel, where I will build an altar to the God who answered my prayers when I was in distress. He has been with me wherever I have gone.' So they gave Jacob all their pagan idols and earrings, and he buried them under the great tree near Shechem.* (Genesis 35:2–4)

# Accounted For

He pointed to the book. It lay open on the desktop, and he used his large hands to swivel it round until it faced her.

'What are they counting?' she asked.

'Your tears,' he replied.

*You keep track of all my sorrows.*
*You have collected all my tears in your bottle.*
*You have recorded each one in your book.*
(Psalm 56:8)

# Vari

The stones were so white. They were so white that Vari squinted at their brightness. She stepped closer and ran her hand over one, her fingers brushing over the words etched into the white stone.

They were just as God had instructed the Israelites. He had instructed them, down to the finest of details, about what they must do when they crossed the Jordan River and took possession of their land.

They were to choose the stones, plaster the stones, and write his instructions on their face, so Vari and her community would never forget them. They had done it all, followed his every command.

Vari stood back again, admiring their size, their height and their width. They shone in the sunlight, rays of light bringing their words to life, as though God himself shone a spotlight on their surface.

Vari was glad she had come to Mount Ebal, to stand before the stones, and she could see now why he had instructed them to be made. Vari could see that with the work and attention that had gone into creating them, her people would be drawn here, to read his instructions, to gaze at their brilliant white and to remember their God who had saved them.

'Thank you for your words,' she whispered to him.

*When you cross the Jordan River and enter the land the Lord your God is giving you, set up some large stones and coat them with plaster. Write this whole body of instruction on them when you cross the river to enter the land the Lord your God is giving you—a land flowing with milk and honey, just as the Lord, the God of your ancestors, promised you. When you cross the Jordan, set up these stones at Mount Ebal and coat them with plaster, as I am commanding you today.* (Deuteronomy 27:2–4)

# A Signet Ring

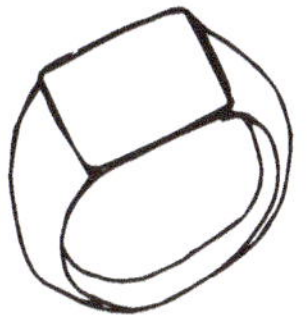

Joseph looked down to the signet ring on his finger. His hand was trembling, and he hoped nobody else could see. The skin on his hands looked brand new to Joseph. Fresh and scrubbed clean for the first time in so long. It had been a lifetime since he had been showered like this.

Only that very morning, Joseph had woken up in the darkness of his prison cell, as he did every morning. Here he was now, just hours later, standing in Pharaoh's court before the king of Egypt. Not only did he stand before the king; he now wore the king's signet ring. The ring was still warm from Pharaoh's own hand.

Joseph stood as still as a statue, barely breathing, as a gold necklace was fastened around his neck. He tried his hardest to concentrate on what Pharaoh was saying. Joseph had only come here today to listen to a dream, after being summoned by the king and desperately praying to God that he might reveal the dream's meaning to Joseph.

God had been with him today, as he had been since the moment Joseph had arrived here in Egypt many years ago. God was for Joseph, not against him. Joseph knew this now—in this moment, more than ever before.

'I hereby put you in charge of the entire land of Egypt.' Pharaoh spoke directly to Joseph.

Should he reply?

No. He remained silent, waiting and listening. God had

whispered to Joseph about the meaning of Pharaoh's dreams today. In the same way, he whispered to Joseph now, telling Joseph not to fear, telling him, 'step into what I have for you.'

'I am Pharaoh,' Pharaoh declared. 'But no one will lift a hand or a foot throughout the entire land of Egypt without your approval,' he said to Joseph. The power he transferred to Joseph in this one simple sentence was simply astonishing.

*Then Pharaoh said to Joseph, 'Since God has revealed the meaning of the dreams to you, clearly no one else is as intelligent or wise as you are. You will be in charge of my court and all my people will take orders from you. Only I, sitting on my throne, will have a rank higher than yours.'*

*Pharaoh said to Joseph, 'I hereby put you in charge of the entire land of Egypt.' Then Pharaoh removed his signet ring from his hand and placed it on Joseph's finger. He dressed him in fine linen clothing and hung a gold chain around his neck. (Genesis 41:39–42)*

When my heart breaks for my child's pain and my eyes fill with tears and I remember that you know. Because you watched your child in pain too.


*Since he did not spare even his own Son but gave him up for us all, won't he also give us everything else?*
(Romans 8:32)

# Hope

God watched Jesus from his vantage point. He watched as Jesus walked through the grainfields. He watched as Jesus explained to the Pharisees why his disciples were allowed to eat there. He watched as Jesus healed in the synagogue, restoring a hand to its former glory and as he spoke quietly to those who opposed him.

God whispered to Jesus of the meeting that was called, to plot against his life. He watched as Jesus moved on from that area. He watched the crowds that followed him. He watched as Jesus healed the sick among the crowds and as he warned them not to reveal who he really was. He watched the hearts of those who heard Jesus and saw how their hearts were transformed, and saw their hope transferred to his Son.

*Look at my Servant, whom I have chosen. He is my Beloved, who pleases me.*

*I will put my Spirit upon him, and he will proclaim justice to the nations.*

*He will not fight or shout or raise his voice in public.*

*He will not crush the weakest reed or put out a flickering candle. Finally he will cause justice to be victorious.*

*And his name will be the hope of all the world.* (Matthew 12:18–21)

# The Lion of Judah

Their father was dying. Judah and his brothers gathered around his bed. Judah had eleven brothers, and they stood together now, shoulder to shoulder, all eyes on their father. Judah would miss Jacob. Though their relationship had been strained at times, Judah loved his father very much. He could barely believe that his time had already come. Judah was silent. They all were. They waited to hear what their father would say. God was with Jacob, and because of this, he was a very wise man.

'Gather around me so that I can tell you about what will happen to each of you in the years to come,' Jacob told his sons. His voice was raspy and barely a whisper, but the brothers were so still, and so quiet, they hung on his every word.

Jacob began with Reuben. He was the oldest, after all. Judah wouldn't have to wait long for his turn because Judah was Jacob's fourth son. His heartbeat pounded against his chest as he listened to Jacob move from Reuben to Simeon and to Levi. Though some of their fathers' words were harsh, Jacob said them in such a way that Judah's older brothers simply wept and squeezed their father's hands inside their own. Jacob loved his sons, and his eyes as he spoke to each of them now stood testimony to this fact.

Finally, Jacob turned to Judah. Judah held his breath. His father looked into his eyes for what seemed like a long time. Judah shuffled from one foot to the other. He didn't know whether to fear or anticipate his father's words. He simply had no idea what they would be. Judah was acutely aware that his future hung on whatever his father said next.

'Judah.' Jacob paused, as though taking in the entirety of his son. Nothing could have prepared Judah for what his father said next.

'Your brothers will praise you.' They were five simple words and Jacob confirmed them with a nod. There was a stirring in the room, and Judah's eyes widened as his father's life-giving words washed over him.

'You will grasp your enemies by their necks. All of your relatives will bow down before you,' Jacob went on, and Judah felt the blood drain from his face. All eyes were on Judah. He knew it. He could feel their eyes, even though he hadn't looked around.

'Judah.' His father paused again, and the corners of his mouth rose slightly. Tears filled Judah's eyes. 'My son is a young lion that has finished eating its prey. He crouches and lies down. Like a lioness, who dares to wake him?' It wasn't a question, but it hung in the room just the same. Jacob took a deep breath.

'The sceptre will not be taken from Judah, nor the ruler's staff be taken from his descendants, until the coming of the one who it belongs to, the one whom all nations will honour.'

Judah inhaled sharply. He had lost all composure now, and it didn't matter that his brothers heard him. After all, they could hear their father's words as clearly as Judah could. There were no secrets here.

But Judah could not believe what his father had said. Could his words be true? Was there someone coming in Judah's line who all the nations would honour? But why? What had Judah done to have been chosen for such an honour?

And there was more—Jacob hadn't finished yet. 'He ties his foal to a grapevine, the colt of his donkey to a vine. He washes his clothes in wine, his robes in the blood of grapes. His eyes are darker than wine, and his teeth are whiter than milk.'

Judah stood, blinking unbelieving eyes. He could hardly breathe. His mouth hung wide open. He could feel it, but was simply unable to close it.

Suddenly, Judah saw a man, somewhere deep in his mind's eye. The man was familiar, but Judah didn't know him. There were similarities though. The man looked a little like Judah, and a little like Judah's own sons. But he had darker eyes than Judah, eyes darker than a well-aged wine. And his teeth were so white, whiter than pure milk. He rode on a donkey, and his clothes were red, like blood.

So red were his clothes … as though they had been washed in blood.

*Then Jacob called together all his sons and said, 'Gather around me, and I will tell you what will happen to each of you in the days to come.'*

*Judah, my son, is a young lion that has finished eating its prey. Like a lion he crouches and lies down; like a lioness—who dares to rouse him? The sceptre will not depart from Judah, nor the ruler's staff from his descendants, until the coming of the one to whom it belongs, the one whom all nations will honour. He ties his foal to a grapevine, the colt of his donkey to a choice vine. He washes his clothes in wine, his robes in the blood of grapes. His eyes are darker than wine, and his teeth are whiter than milk.*
(Genesis 49:1,9–12)

# Security

She sat in his shadow, but it was not cold here. His was no ordinary shadow. The temperature here was perfect, and she was safe. Joy consumed her. There was a wall to her right, and she leaned her head against it. The wall was soft and warm because it was made of flesh. The wall was his hand. She clung to his hand, the hand of her helper, and she opened her mouth to express her joy.

It came out in a song.

*I lie awake thinking of you,*
*meditating on you through the night.*
*Because you are my helper,*
*I sing for joy in the shadow of your wings.*
*I cling to you;*
*your strong right hand holds me securely.*
(Psalm 63:6–8)

# Waters

The sea beside Pi-hahiroth was a special place. The waters there were set apart. Their story had always been a part of his story, though not yet written. But because the waters belonged to him and because the waters were listening, they were waiting.

The space was sacred.

Visitors could feel it beside the sea of Pi-hahiroth, and today Moses was visiting. He stood beside the sea along with hundreds of thousands of Israelites.

The waters listened as the people panicked. Their oppressors approached with raised fists and death in their eyes as the Israelite people trembled beside the sea.

'Why did you bring us here? We will surely die in the wilderness!' they cried out to Moses in fear. 'Were there not more than enough graves for us back in Egypt? What have you done? Why did you make us leave? We told you this would happen while we were still in Egypt? We told you, 'Just leave us alone! Let us be slaves. It is better to be a slave here in Egypt than to be dead out in the wilderness!'

The waters watched Moses carefully. He did not panic. Could this be the time they had waited for? Would the sacred waters beside Pi-hahiroth be written into his story today?

'Do not be scared,' Moses's voice rang out over the crowd. 'Just be still and watch the Lord rescue you. The Lord will save you today and the Egyptians you see now will never be seen again. The Lord will fight for you today. Just stay calm.'

Just. Stay. Calm.

Three simple words, but they were the words the waters had been waiting for. Today, the waters beside Pi-hahiroth would do something new. Today, the waters would get out of the way, creating a space for the escape of God's people.

*The Egyptians caught up with the people of Israel as they were camped beside the shore near Pi-hahiroth, across from Baal-zephon. As Pharaoh approached, the people of Israel looked up and panicked when they saw the Egyptians overtaking them. They cried out to the Lord. But Moses told the people, 'Don't be afraid. Just stand still and watch the Lord rescue you today. The Egyptians you see today will never be seen again. The Lord himself will fight for you. Just stay calm.' (Exodus 14:9–10,13–14)*

# Zulei

Zulei had felt guilty over the years, but not guilty enough to actually confess to her husband. No, she would never do that. It had been many years since the incident, and though the guilt followed her around like a dark cloud, she knew Joseph was in prison now. She would never have to see him again or deal with the consequences of her actions.

Some days, when Zulei thought over what had happened, it felt like she was looking at somebody else's life. Zulei had matured, grown up since then, and she was surprised at herself when she remembered the way she had behaved toward Joseph … surprised and embarrassed.

Joseph had worked for Zulei's husband Potiphar for a number of years, and Zulei had been attracted to him in all the wrong ways. She was a married woman, after all. Zulei was beautiful and she knew it. She was sure that Joseph thought so. But he had embarrassed her when she'd made her intentions clear, and in turn, she had lied about him.

Zulei had told her husband, an extremely powerful man in Egypt, that Joseph had tried to have his way with her. Joseph had been in prison ever since. It had been many years.

Zulei often remembered what had happened with Joseph when she and Potiphar were here, inside Pharaoh's palace, because she knew Joseph lived in the prison beneath the palace, right beneath where they stood.

Today, Pharaoh was distressed and had called a meeting. Zulei stood close beside her husband and watched with shock as Joseph stepped into the room where they gathered. Joseph stood before Pharaoh's throne. Potiphar stiffened noticeably beside Zulei, and she felt her heart in the back of her throat at the sight of Joseph. She reached out a hand and held it on her husband's back. The hand was as much to steady herself as it was for her husband. The room swayed around her as Pharaoh's words rang out.

Joseph's God had spoken to Joseph, had helped Pharaoh, had rescued Joseph … Joseph would be released from prison on this very day… Joseph would rule over all of Egypt… Nobody would demand more respect than Joseph besides Pharaoh himself.

Zulei couldn't breathe. It was clear to everybody in the room that Joseph's God was with him. That Joseph was a holy man.

Potiphar looked back into Zulei's eyes. Then, for the first time since Joseph had been sent to prison, Zulei saw something that sent shivers down her spine. Something she had never seen there before … suspicion. Fear welled up inside her until tears pricked her eyes and her guilt spilled over, betraying her.

There was no hiding now.

*Joseph was a very handsome and well-built young man, and Potiphar's wife soon began to look at him lustfully. 'Come and sleep with me,' she demanded.*

*But Joseph refused. 'Look,' he told her, 'my master trusts me with everything in his entire household. No one here has more authority than I do. He has held back nothing from me except you, because you are his wife. How could I do such a wicked thing? It would be a great sin against God.'* (Genesis 39:6–9)

# The Beginning

He brushed down the shittim wood and placed his chisel on the workbench beside the wood. It was almost finished now, but he needed to sleep. Today had been a long day in the workshop, and his eyelids had grown heavy as the daylight disappeared. He rose from his stool, stretched his arms up high above his head, and yawned out loud as he swept his eyes over the workshop. Not too messy this evening—nothing that couldn't wait for the morning. He fetched his tunic from the hook on the door and headed out back to rest.

*After his baptism, as Jesus came up out of the water, the heavens were opened and he saw the Spirit of God descending like a dove and settling on him. And a voice from heaven said, 'This is my dearly loved Son, who brings me great joy.'* (Matthew 3:16–17)

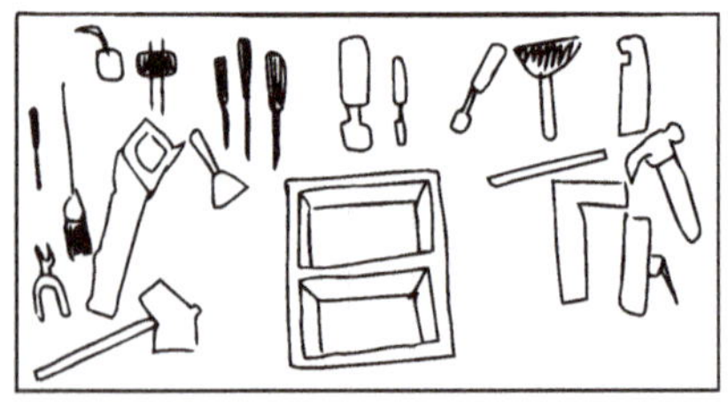

Thank you for wanting me.


*He chose to give birth to us by giving us his true word. And we, out of all creation, became his prized possession.* (James 1:18)

# Water Transport

'Go south,' the voice had whispered.

Philip had not hesitated, not even for a moment. Now he walked down the desert road that ran between Jerusalem and Gaza. There was a carriage up ahead of Philip, and it sounded like somebody inside was reading aloud.

'Go and walk beside the carriage.' The whispered instructions were clear and calm, and Philip followed each one as soon as he heard it. He quietly drew up beside the carriage, adjusting his pace to match its speed, walking in step with it and listening.

'He was led like a sheep to be slaughtered,' the man inside read aloud. 'And as a lamb stays silent before the shearers, he did not speak.'

Excitement bubbled within Philip's belly, because Philip recognised the words. He knew them well. The man in the carriage was reading from the Book of Isaiah.

'He was humiliated and was given no justice,' the man read on. 'No one can speak of his descendants because his life was taken from him.'

The traveller's voice trailed off and there was quiet inside the carriage. Blood pumped through Philip's ears and his heart raced as he realised it was time for him to speak now. He took a deep breath…

'Do you have understanding about what you are reading?' Philip called, loud enough to be heard over the carriage wheels. Suddenly, the carriage stopped, and so did Philip. The curtain was drawn aside and out popped a man's head. He looked Philip up and down, clearly surprised. What would he say to Philip? Would he tell him to go away? Would he ask why he was listening to his private reading?

'Well, how can I?' the man finally asked. 'Unless someone teaches me about it?' He beckoned for Philip to jump up and join him. Philip let out the breath he had been holding and stepped up into the carriage and sat beside the man.

It didn't take Philip long to recognise the traveller—he was the treasurer of Ethiopia! A eunuch of great authority under the Kandake, the queen of Ethiopia. God had clearly led Philip straight to the eunuch. Philip didn't let it bother him. He would speak to the eunuch as though he were speaking to anybody else. God had sent him here, after all.

'So please tell me, was the writer speaking about himself or was he speaking about somebody else?' the eunuch asked.

'He was not speaking about himself but about somebody else.' Philip saw his opportunity. 'And I know who it was.' Philip wasn't expecting the emotion to be so close to the surface. He blinked away his tears and cleared his throat. Beginning with the scripture the eunuch had been reading, Philip told him about Jesus. It wasn't hard for him to speak about Jesus because Philip knew it was the truth with all of his heart.

But the way of Jesus could be hard to hear … unless the Spirit helped, unless the Spirit opened the eunuch's eyes. Philip flung his arms around the carriage, wrapped up in his storytelling, as he told of Jesus's baptism, of the way he was silent before his accusers, of his death and his resurrection. Before he knew it, the eunuch's face was streaked with tears and a mixture of fear and wonder which Philip completely understood.

The eunuch jumped to his feet without warning.

'Please stop the carriage now,' he called out.

The carriage came to an abrupt halt.

The eunuch pointed out the window. 'Look! We are passing by water. Can I be baptised right now?'

Philip could hardly believe what was happening as he followed the man down from the carriage and strode out beside him into the water. He could hardly believe it, but at the same time, of course this was happening.

Philip smiled at the eunuch as he wrapped his arm over his shoulder. The Spirit drew near as Philip proceeded to dunk the man beneath the surface.

The instant Philip's arms came back up out of the water, he was transported somewhere else, to a different place. The river had disappeared, but his arms were still wet. He lifted his hands and ran them through his hair.

Philip now sat in a bathtub. He was no longer outside, and there was no eunuch. He jumped up from the tub and flung his legs over its side. He wrapped a towel around his waist and peered out of the room's only window, trying to figure out where he was.

He looked down the road to the left and to the right. Nothing looked familiar. He spotted a sign beside the road.

Azotus.

With the Spirit's help, he had travelled in the blink of an eye to the town of Azotus. Clearly, God had work for Philip to do here now.

*When they came up out of the water, the Spirit of the Lord snatched Philip away. The eunuch never saw him again but went on his way rejoicing. Meanwhile, Philip found himself farther north at the town of Azotus. He preached the Good News there and in every town along the way until he came to Caesarea.* (Acts 8:39–40)

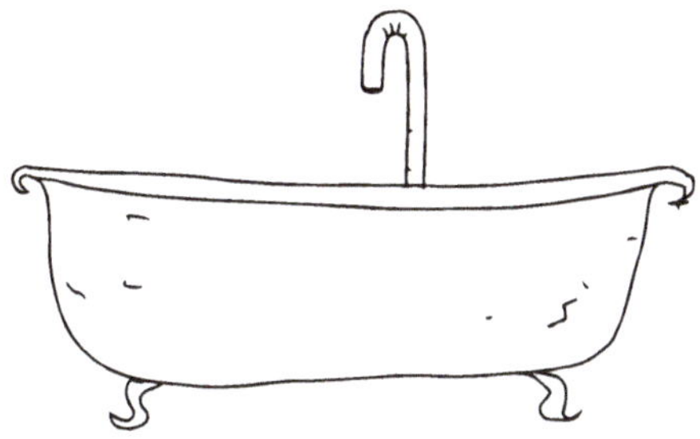

# Listen

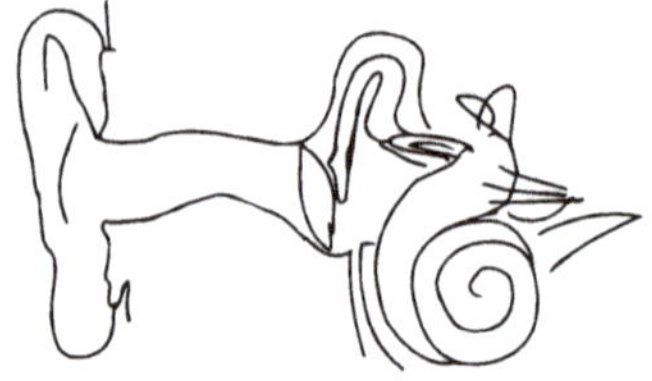

Deep within the ear canal, where silence had always lived, there was a sound.

'Be opened,' the words whispered. They were two simple words and the inner ear stood to attention with the movement of them. A vibration that had never occurred here before. The words ran down the walls lining the deep passage; they ran down through the walls that led to the eardrum, the walls comprised of skin and bone. The ear did something new.

For the first time since the day of its creation, it listened.

For the first time since its creation, it heard.

*A deaf man with a speech impediment was brought to him, and the people begged Jesus to lay his hands on the man to heal him.*

*Jesus led him away from the crowd so they could be alone. He put his fingers into the man's ears. Then, spitting on his own fingers, he touched the man's tongue. Looking up to heaven, he sighed and said, 'Ephphatha,' which means, 'Be opened!' Instantly the man could hear perfectly, and his tongue was freed so he could speak plainly!* (Mark 7:32–35)

# Esme

Esme stood very still, with her feet planted firmly on the ground … or were they? She watched her feet now. They were her feet—she recognised them, though they appeared more youthful than they had been before she'd arrived here.

Esme stood on the grass. She could feel it poking up between her toes, but she could see the grass not only between her toes but beneath her feet as well. Were her feet see-through? That was impossible. And though she stood on the ground, she also seemed to float just above it … somehow.

Esme felt light. Not only did she feel light, but light was all she could see. The purest, most breathtaking light. It surrounded her and shone through every blade of grass under her feet and every flower that towered over her head. The light shone through Esme, too.

It wasn't a light that came from the sun. Esme knew that without being told. The light that shone here, the light that shone through everything in this place, came from Jesus.

There was no joy on earth that came close to the bubbling joy that Esme felt now. An all-consuming joy, brimming up to overflowing, streamed through Esme's spirit. There was nothing that compared to this.

Was Esme home? She had never been here before, but now that she was here, she never wanted to leave this place. There were things to go back for, people Esme loved on earth, but her memories of them seemed far off, like they were a dream and this was real. This was ecstasy.

She couldn't leave now she had tasted it. Esme floated forward beneath the towering flowers, their colours indescribable, unearthly, their scent heavenly. Esme was accepted here, and she could feel the love.

Esme was known here, and she was loved.

Then Esme saw something far off, in the distance. Had it been there all along? It was a city that shone so bright. Esme was drawn to it like nothing else. She instinctively knew he was there. As though his throne called out to her and she longed to go towards the city. To find him there.

'Surely this is our God,' she whispered to herself as she stepped through the grass at her feet. 'We trusted in our God, and now he has saved us.'

Esme headed toward the golden city.

*In Jerusalem, the Lord of Heaven's Armies will spread a wonderful feast for all the people of the world.*

*It will be a delicious banquet with clear, well-aged wine and choice meat.*

*There he will remove the cloud of gloom, the shadow of death that hangs over the earth.*

*He will swallow up death forever! The Sovereign Lord will wipe away all tears.*

*He will remove forever all insults and mockery against his land and people. The Lord has spoken.*

*In that day the people will proclaim, 'This is our God! We trusted in him, and he saved us! This is the Lord in whom we trusted. Let us rejoice in the salvation he brings!'*
(Isaiah 25:6–9)

Would you change my heart?
Would you give me a new heart?


*The Lord your God will change your heart and the hearts
of all your descendants, so that you will love him with all
your heart and soul and so you may live!*
(Deuteronomy 30:6)

# Half Mile

John was reeling. He bounded up the last few steps into the upstairs room at the house where they were staying. It had only been ten minutes since he had stood on the Mount of Olives with his neck stretched back, watching as Jesus disappeared. He had watched Jesus rise into the sky with his own eyes. John and the others. It had really happened. They had really seen it.

There were strangers who stood amongst them too—more of them than usual on the Mount of Olives. And the strangers were not from this world.

'Men of Galilee,' one had called, addressing John and the others. 'Why are you just standing here and staring up into the sky?'

Though John's mouth hung open, he did not reply and neither did anybody else.

'Jesus has been taken from you and he is now in heaven,' the angel went on. 'But one day he will come back from heaven. He will return in the same way that you saw him leave!'

*Then the apostles returned to Jerusalem from the Mount of Olives, a distance of half a mile. When they arrived, they went to the upstairs room of the house where they were staying.* (Acts 1:12–13)

# The Great Rock

God placed a great rock in Jerusalem.

The rock was Jesus.

Many tripped up on this rock. They didn't want to build their homes on its foundation. Instead, they believed they must work hard to be worthy of the rock.

But God told those who would listen, 'Build your home on this rock. Use this rock as the foundation for your life. You can access this foundation by believing that you are forgiven, that my grace is enough for you.'

It was hard for the people to have faith, to truly believe their mistakes were not held against them.

But some of the people did believe.

These were the people who believed God did not point a finger at them and condemn them.

These were the people who denied the enemy's invitation to feel guilty, who recognised the enemy had no place on this rock.

These were the people who built their homes with the rock as their foundation.

These were the people who belonged to Jesus.

*What does all this mean? Even though the Gentiles were not trying to follow God's standards, they were made right with God. And it was by faith that this took place.*

*But the people of Israel, who tried so hard to get right with God by keeping the law, never succeeded. Why not? Because they were trying to get right with God by keeping the law instead of by trusting in him. They stumbled over the great rock in their path. God warned them of this in the Scriptures when he said,*

*'I am placing a stone in Jerusalem that makes people stumble, a rock that makes them fall. But anyone who trusts in him will never be disgraced.'* (Romans 9:30–33)

# Dia

Sometimes Dia let herself think about when she, Synty, and Clement had spent their days together. She thought back to happier times when the three of them had been the greatest of friends, travelling together, passionately telling the people of the hope they had found.

But not any more.

Dia still had hope—she still had Jesus—but she no longer had a friendship with Synty. Their friendship had ended abruptly, and—though she wouldn't admit it—Dia struggled to pinpoint exactly what had gone wrong between them. She wondered if Synty remembered the details of their disagreement; she wondered if she had offended Synty in some way unknowingly. But for the most part, Dia tried not to think of Synty at all; some days this was easier than others and today was not one of them.

The believers had gathered to hear the reading of Paul's letter. Paul was their founder, and his letters were few and far between, so everybody was eager to hear from him. Dia had been tempted to miss the meeting to avoid being in the same room as Synty. Instead, she'd made sure she arrived early, and positioned herself beside the wall, close to the front of the room, so she could easily avoid eye contact with her. Though Dia couldn't see Synty, she recognised her voice the moment that she arrived. The sound of her laughter sent prickles up Dia's spine. She wished she hadn't come.

Tom stood up to address those gathered. Phew, the letter would be read now. Then Dia could duck out as soon as it was over. Tom cleared his throat.

'Here goes.' He winked at them all. There was excitement in the air, and Tom was as excited as the rest of them. Dia had been excited too, but that was before her fallout with Synty. In fact, much of Día's joy had dimmed since their falling out. She sighed and turned her attention to Tom.

'I pray that your love will bubble up and overflow more and more, and that you will grow both in knowledge and in understanding. I want you to understand what actually matters, so that your lives may be pure and blameless until the day that Christ Jesus returns,' Tom read.

Paul's words touched a part of Dia, deep down inside of her being. She let them wash over her as she was reminded of Jesus and his love for her, of God's promise, of her reason.

'So do not worry about anything,' Tom read on, 'but instead pray about everything.' Tom bounced from one foot to the other, his excitement evident, and Dia smiled to herself. 'Tell God about the things that you need and then thank him for all he has already done.'

There was movement around Dia, as though the room came alive with Paul's words. Those beside her nodded their heads in agreement, shifting in their seats, excitement bubbling.

'This way you will experience the peace of God, his peace exceeds our understanding. His peace guards our hearts and our minds as we live in him.'

Tom paused for a moment as though reading on ahead to himself. He glanced up awkwardly, taking in the room, his eyes met Dia's just for a moment before dropping back down to the letter. Dia shifted uncomfortably. What was this? She sensed a shift in Tom's mood.

'Now.' He cleared his throat and briefly paused again. 'I write to Dia and Synty.' Tom's words caught Dia off guard and the noise in the room instantly quietened around her. The room was still. Dia froze in her seat and could feel the eyes behind her. She concentrated on her breathing, in and out, in and out. She could not believe Paul had written about their argument. What would the letter say next?

'Because you belong to God, please make peace with one another and settle your disagreement.' Tom's voice was pained as he read on, and he didn't look up again, as though he wanted to get the words out, to get it over with, as much as Dia did. 'I ask that you, my faithful friend, would please help these women, for they both worked with me in telling others the Good News about Jesus Christ. They worked hard together with Clement and the rest of our co-workers. Their names are recorded in the Book of Life.'

Dia could hear her heartbeat throbbing in her ears. The room grew silent. What was Synty thinking? Should Dia turn around and look at her? She didn't want to, but Paul cared about them, and Dia could feel the Holy Spirit weaving through his letter.

There was a sob from the back of the room. Dia recognised the sound. She spun on her seat. Tears streamed down Synty's face. No sooner had Dia looked into Synty's eyes than the two girls jumped to their feet, crossed the room, and embraced. Synty's hair hid Dia from the seated crowd and the girls sobbed, holding each other.

Their feud was finally over.


*Now I appeal to Euodia and Syntyche. Please, because you belong to the Lord, settle your disagreement. And I ask you, my true partner, to help these two women, for they worked hard with me in telling others the Good News. They worked along with Clement and the rest of my co-workers, whose names are written in the Book of Life.* (Philippians 4:2–3)

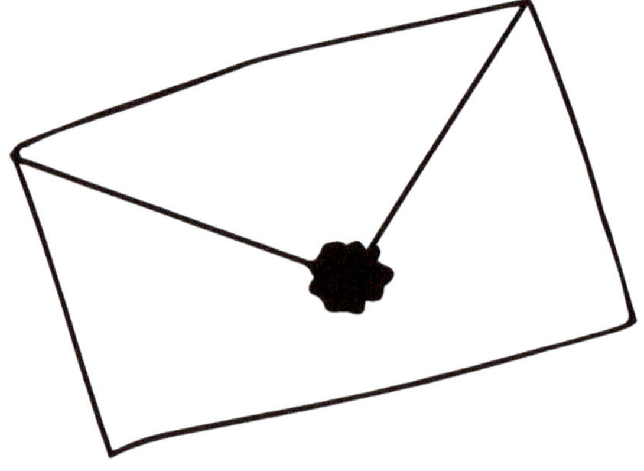

# Hopelessness

How do I pick myself up from here?
I don't know where to turn to.
Please come near.
Please rescue me.
Because you are my hero, Lord. You always are.


*For the Lord your God is living among you. He is a mighty saviour. He will take delight in you with gladness. With his love, he will calm all your fears. He will rejoice over you with joyful songs. (Zephaniah 3:17)*

# Eli

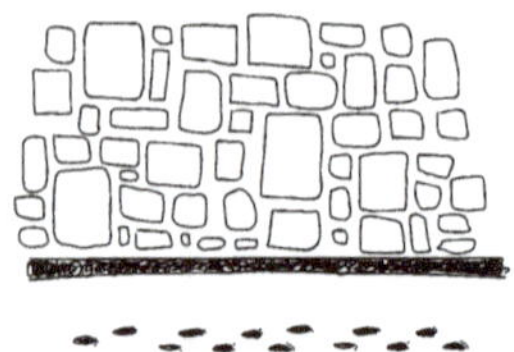

Eli had been having a hard time sleeping recently. He wondered if it was due to his bad eyesight. His eyes no longer worked the way they once had. Eli was very old, and it seemed his eyes were too.

Eli could barely see any more, and his days were spent with very little movement. He wondered if his quiet days were the reason he struggled to fall asleep when night came, because his energy was not spent. He often found himself lying awake, sometimes for hours on end, while the world around him slept.

But tonight, Eli was pleased to discover his body felt tired. He had spent some time on his feet during the day. Now his head rested on his pillow, he could tell that—for tonight, at least—sleep would come easily.

Before long, Eli felt the sweet beginnings of sleep melting over him. He was right on the verge of sleep, in the space between awareness and slumber, when Eli heard a voice.

It was Samuel.

'Here I am,' Samuel said from the doorway to Eli's bedroom. 'You called me?'

'I didn't say a word.' Eli tried to keep the annoyance from his voice. 'Go back to bed,' he told the boy.

Samuel turned on his heel immediately and went back to bed. Eli listened to his footsteps as they disappeared down the hall. He was a good boy. Always obedient … unlike Eli's own sons. His thoughts turned to his boys as he sank back into his pillow. Though the worry for his sons often kept his mind from settling, tonight he was tired. Soon, waves of sleepiness again drifted over him. Again, just as his awareness verged on surrender to the waves, Samuel was back in his doorway.

'Here I am. Why did you call?' he asked again.

Eli's eyes flung back open and his heart raced, he'd been more asleep than awake that time.

'I did not call, my son.' Eli wanted to tell Samuel not to bother him again, but before he could say anything, Samuel was off, plodding back to his bed mat.

Eli lay awake for a little longer this time. What had Samuel heard that he mistook for Eli's voice? Was there an animal scrummaging around outside? Had one of the servants been calling his name? Eli didn't know, but he hoped the boy had drifted off to sleep now so he could too!

'I am here. Did you call me?' Eli's eyes sprang open once again.

Right. That was it, he sat up on his bed mat and turned towards Samuel. This was beyond a joke now. But suddenly Eli was struck with a thought. Was the Lord speaking to Samuel?

No.

Surely not?

But could it have been?

Something in Eli's spirit pushed him on. Tears sprang to Eli's eyes, and the realisation swept over him. It had been the Lord. The Lord was calling to Samuel. Eli realised he'd been silent for some time, and Samuel was waiting.

Eli cleared his throat, battling to keep the emotion from his voice.

'Go back to your bed and when you lie down, if someone calls to you, say, "Speak, Lord, for I am listening."' Eli couldn't see the expression on Samuel's face, but he could imagine it. Samuel paused for a moment and let out a breath as though he'd been holding it, then he turned and walked back to his bed, as Eli had commanded.

*Samuel did not yet know the Lord because he had never had a message from the Lord before. So the Lord called a third time, and once more Samuel got up and went to Eli. 'Here I am. Did you call me?' Then Eli realised it was the Lord who was calling the boy. So he said to Samuel, 'Go and lie down again, and if someone calls again, say, "Speak, Lord, your servant is listening."' So Samuel went back to bed.* (1 Samuel 3:7–10)

Simply believe.

*God saved you by his grace when you believed. And you can't take credit for this; it is a gift from God. Salvation is not a reward for the good things we have done, so none of us can boast about it.* (Ephesians 2:8–9)

# Night Lights

The stars were silent. But that was enough.

They need not cry out or strive for attention; they need not cry out to make their presence known.

They were silent and they were many, their light bringing the night sky to life, bringing creation to its knees with their mystery, with their beauty.

Their majesty was no secret, their creator on display—one need only look up to behold them.

*The heavens proclaim the glory of God.*
*The skies display his craftmanship.*
*Day after day they continue to speak;*
*night after night they make him known.*
*They speak without a sound or word;*
*their voice is never heard.*
*Yet their message has gone throughout the earth,*
*and their words to all the world.*
(Psalm 19:1–4)

# Toffi

Toffi stood beside Mamma and Pappa in a big crowd, listening to Moses. Toffi was only eight years old, and she couldn't understand much of what Moses was saying. But she could hear the passion in his voice, and she understood some of it.

Toffi understood that their God, the God of Israel, had rescued her people from slavery in Egypt. Toffi's God had kept them safe and fed them and led them through the wilderness for many years, before Toffi was even born. And now Toffi's God had prepared a home for the Israelites.

Their new home sounded wonderful to Toffi. God told them about how it flowed with milk and honey. But now, as Toffi stood before Moses and listened to him read out God's instructions, Toffi wondered about the instructions. Were the instructions simply the way God wanted the Israelites to behave? Or were they more about keeping the Israelites safe? Toffi didn't know. But she listened to every word and tried her best to place each one.

'The Lord has secrets and nobody knows what they are,' Moses called out.

Toffi was leaning against her Mama, but she stood straight up when she heard this. God had secrets? Toffi had secrets too! But she'd never considered that God might have them. What might God's secrets be?

'We are not accountable for these secrets,' Moses went on. 'But we and our children are accountable forever for all that God has made known to us, so we must obey all of his instructions.'

Toffi tried to keep up, but this was harder to understand. She pulled on her father's hand until he leaned down beside her.

Toffi cupped her hand over her father's ear.

'I heard him say "children",' she whispered proudly to her father. He nodded at Toffi and ruffled her hair as he quickly stood back up again.

Moses kept speaking, but Toffi was daydreaming now. She thought of the milk and the honey, longing for it. If only she could taste some of the honey today. There were so many children. Would there be enough honey to go around? Would she get to try some?

Suddenly, Moses's voice changed and Toffi's attention snapped back to him. Was Moses crying? No. Not quite, but Toffi thought he might start to. His face was so red, and his arms were waving up and down, this way and that, with each word he spoke.

'Today I am giving you a choice. It is a choice between life and death, a choice between blessings and curses,' Moses called out.

Toffi could feel his every word, as though each one was placed inside her chest.

'I call on heaven and earth to witness the choice you make. Oh, that you might choose life.' His voice cracked.

Toffi had been right. Moses was crying.

'So that you and your descendants will live.' It was clear that Moses cared deeply for God's words, the words he shared with the Israelites.

Toffi wanted to choose life! She desperately wanted to. The crowd were still and quiet. Toffi held her breath in case it would be too loud. There was a long pause. Was Moses finished?

No.

'You make this choice by loving the Lord, by obeying his words, and by committing your whole self to him, for good.' His voice was quieter now, and it sounded raspy. 'This is the key to your whole life. If you love the Lord and if you obey him, you will live long in the land that he promised to your ancestors, Abraham, Isaac, and Jacob.'

The land that was flowing with milk and honey, Toffi thought to herself.

*Therefore, obey the terms of this covenant so that you will prosper in everything you do. All of you—tribal leaders, elders, officers, all the men of Israel—are standing today in the presence of the Lord your God. Your little ones and your wives are with you, as well as the foreigners living among you who chop your wood and carry your water. You are standing here today to enter into the covenant of the Lord your God. (Deuteronomy 29:9–12)*

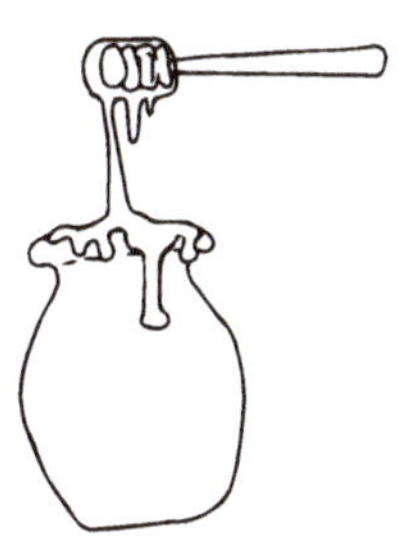

# Why 

Why do you let me come here? Why am I welcome in your home?

Is it because of the kind way I treat people when I am in a good mood? Is that why you welcome me here?

Or is it because sometimes I am generous with what you have given me?

Is it because occasionally I forgive quickly or because, some weeks, I remember to talk to you throughout my days? Perhaps it's because I sing to you, or because I sometimes remember to ask for your advice?

Is it because of my guilt? Do you pity me because I cannot get it right? Is it because no matter how hard I try, my sin follows me?

Is it because of me that I am welcome here, Lord?

Or is it because of you? Is it because of your unfailing love that I can come here? Because of your unfailing love, I can enter your house.

*Because of your unfailing love,*
*I can enter your house;*
*I will worship at your Temple with deepest awe.*
(Psalm 5:7)

# Mercy

Jesus sat at the long wooden table in Matthew's home. There were no spare seats, because Matthew had invited many people to his dinner party. Jesus leaned back in his chair, observing those around him, listening to their conversations and belly laughs.

There were many tax collectors present—Jesus could tell who they were. He watched some women who sat together towards the end of the table. They were prostitutes—Jesus knew. There was a man who sat across from Jesus and spoke loudly to his companion. The man was a robber who'd also committed murder—and Jesus knew.

Jesus saw a couple, husband and wife, sitting beside each other but barely speaking to one another. They had been cast out of the synagogue. She had committed adultery, and her husband was a drunk. And Jesus knew. He knew them all.

Jesus took a sip from his wine glass and placed it back down beside his plate. He helped himself to some of the lamb, thanking God for his meal. The party was loud all around him, and his disciples were enjoying themselves. Each and every person present was exactly where they were meant to be. Jesus took a bite of his lamb from his plate and watched as the people erupted into laughter around the table once again. These were why he had come. He loved them all, each and every one.

*Later, Matthew invited Jesus and his disciples to his home as dinner guests, along with many tax collectors and other disreputable sinners. But when the Pharisees saw this, they asked his disciples, 'Why does your teacher eat with such scum?'*

*When Jesus heard this, he said, 'Healthy people don't need a doctor—sick people do.' Then he added, 'Now go and learn the meaning of this Scripture: "I want you to show mercy, not offer sacrifices." For I have come to call not those who think they are righteous, but those who know they are sinners.'* (Matthew 9:10–13)

# Faith

When I try to be perfect to be accepted by you … I fail.
As it turns out, I cannot be perfect.
But you tell me:
'When you make your mistakes—come to me.
I will hide you in the shelter of my wings.
I will forgive your mistakes.
All you have to do is believe that I forgive them.
All you have to do is trust me.
Put your faith in me.
You do not have to try to be perfect.'
And then I remember again.
I remember who you are.
I remember the safety beneath your wings.
And I breathe deeply.

*So it is clear that no one can be made right with God by trying to keep the law. For the Scriptures say, 'It is through faith that a righteous person has life.' This way of faith is very different from the way of law, which says, 'It is through obeying the law that a person has life.' But Christ has rescued us from the curse pronounced by the law. When he was hung on the cross, he took upon himself the curse for our wrongdoing. (Galatians 3:11–13)*

You bring life where there was nothing.

144

*Before the mountains were born,*
*before you gave birth to the earth and the world,*
*from beginning to end, you are God.*
(Psalm 90:2)

# Tootu

Tootu the turtle had felt it brewing for a while. He paused his paddling and treaded water as he listened to the ocean calling out. Tootu could hear whales. They were far away, but they belted out their mighty song and it could be heard for many miles. There were dolphins, too. They called out, their whistling coming from all directions. Tootu could hear them from both his left and his right.

The fish joined in as well. There was a mixture of clicking and squeaking and humming and popping, as though every species of fish worked together to shout out their praise. Tootu had felt it brewing and he knew what it was, a mixture of thankfulness and awe. It was a yearning to thank him, their creator.

The ocean came alive all around Tootu, and it seemed that even the water itself breathed his name, the name of their creator. Excitement and wonder stirred up within Tutu, making its way right up to the back of his throat.

Then Tootu called out to him too. Tootu used what he had—he hissed, and he croaked, he grunted and he squealed. Tootu made every noise that he was able, to bring praise to his creator.

*Let the sea and everything in it shout his praise!*
*Let the earth and all living things join in.*

*Let the rivers clap their hands in glee!*
*Let the hills sing out their songs of joy before the Lord.*
(Psalm 98:7–9)

# Dreamer

Peter sat in his prison cell between two soldiers. He wore two chains, and he was hungry and tired. More soldiers stood before him, guarding the prison gate. Why there were so many, he had no idea. Surely they had something better to do—the heavy chains securing him would have been sufficient.

Though he was hungry and though he was tired, he was not afraid. They had killed James last week and would likely kill Peter next. But his hope was firmly rooted in Jesus.

Peter had made the mistake of clutching onto the things of this world before. If the truth be told, he longed to be with Jesus now, though he did wonder if his work on earth was complete. He couldn't be sure.

Instead, he trusted the one who had given him life to begin with. As his eyelids grew heavy, he surrendered to sleep in his prison cell. Peter had not been asleep for long when he had a dream. A man stood before him, but he was no ordinary man. His clothes were bright, and he shone like an angel. It was the most vivid dream Peter had ever had!

'Quickly! Jump up!' the angel told him.

As he spoke, the chains that held Peter fell from his arms. Peter froze, staring down at his arms beside him and then to the chains that lay at his feet. He looked to the guard on his left and then on his right. Would they attack him? Would Peter wake up soon?

'Get dressed and put on your shoes,' the angel instructed.

Peter sprang into action and got dressed as fast as he could. Dream dressing had been difficult in the past, but not today.

'Put on your jacket and follow me,' the angel said.

Peter reached for his jacket and slid an arm in as he followed the angel out the prison gate. They walked straight past one prison guard, then another and another. Finally, they reached the large iron gate that led out to the city. Peter looked to the angel. How would they get through the gate?

But the gate simply opened before their eyes and they were out on the street.

Peter and the angel did not speak but walked side by side. Peter matched the angel's pace, which was almost a run. Then suddenly, the angel was gone. Peter spun on his heel. Where had the angel gone? He had disappeared into thin air and there was only empty space now beside Peter. What on earth?

Peter looked down at his hands. They were calloused and rough, but so very clear. He turned them over, back and forth. What was going on here? And then it dawned on him.

Was he dreaming … or was he awake?

Could this be real? Still looking down at his hands, he slapped himself across the cheek. He jumped up and down and ran both hands through his hair. It was real. He was awake!

'It's really true!' he whispered into the night sky. 'The Lord has sent his angel and he has saved me from Herod and from all that the Jewish leaders had planned to do to me!' Though he spoke the words out loud, his mind was playing catch up, and he could hardly believe they were real.

He was here, he was free, he was standing alone on the street in the middle of the night. Suddenly he remembered the believers. He could go to them now! And with that, he took off down the road to find them, and to unknowingly be the answer to their midnight prayers.

*So Peter left the cell, following the angel. But all the time he thought it was a vision. He didn't realise it was actually happening. They passed the first and second guard posts and came to the iron gate leading to the city, and this opened for them all by itself. So they passed through and started walking down the street, and then the angel suddenly left him.*

*Peter finally came to his senses. 'It's really true!' he said. 'The Lord has sent his angel and saved me from Herod and from what the Jewish leaders had planned to do to me!'*
(Acts 12:9–11)

Life's deep lows.

*Then I pray to you, O Lord.*
*I say, 'You are my place of refuge.*
*You are all I really want in life.*
*Hear my cry, for I am very low.'*
(Psalm 142:5–6)

# Coco

Coco stood in the crowd. There was a man in front of her. His hair was overgrown, and his facial hair was rough and uneven. A woman stood beside him. She swayed from side to side and held her arms over her head, her long golden hair tossing this way and that.

Coco was surrounded by people who gathered before God's throne. It was exactly where she was meant to be. There was a song brewing. The music began and she felt the excitement of the crowd all around her. But Coco didn't recognise the music, so she wouldn't know the words to the song. Though something about the tune did feel familiar … which was odd, because she was sure she had never heard it. But what was that…?

Something bubbled up inside Coco. It travelled from the bottom of her belly, making its way up, weaving through her torso until finally it touched her lips. Coco opened her mouth. She was unsure about what she would sing, but out came the words to a brand new song. A song she had never heard before. She had never heard it, yet the words kept coming, as though she knew the song, as though she had always known it.

Had the words been buried within her all along? Coco looked with shock to the hairy man before her who also sang the new song. He looked back at Coco, his face said it all, a mixture of delight and wonder that he knew the words.

Coco noted the name written on his forehead, the same name written on her own. The hairy man and the entire choir sang together with Coco. They sang the words to a brand new song.

*Then I saw the Lamb standing on Mount Zion, and with him were 144,000 who had his name and his Father's name written on their foreheads. And I heard a sound from heaven like the roar of mighty ocean waves or the rolling of loud thunder. It was like the sound of many harpists playing together. This great choir sang a wonderful new song in front of the throne of God and before the four living beings and the twenty-four elders. No one could learn this song except the 144,000 who had been redeemed from the earth.* (Revelation 14:1–3)

# Face Me

Moses heard a sound. He looked up. Was somebody there? Who was it?

Then Moses saw his face. Moses recognised him. It was his eyes and the shape of his nose, his mouth, and his eyebrows. The colour of his hair and the crease in his forehead. The corners of his lips rose to greet Moses.

Moses had seen his face many, many times, but no matter how many times, it still took his breath away.

Every. Single. Time.

*There has never been another prophet in Israel like Moses, whom the Lord knew face to face.* (Deuteronomy 34:10)

# Dovey

Dovey was the last female dove of her kind to live on planet Earth, and oh, how her life had changed. Dovey no longer lived as she pleased, fluttering from this tree to that and fending for herself when it came to mealtimes.

No, now Dovey lived on a boat, and she was fed by the people, fed at the same time every single day. Dovey missed her old life, her life before the boat that now seemed like a distant memory. She missed taking flight and the freedom it brought.

But now, sitting on Noah's hand as he held it out over the never-ending waters, she was afraid. Noah held his hand out further still, and it was clear what he wanted Dovey to do. It was clear that he wanted her to fly.

But where would she go? There was only water.

Perhaps, if she sat still for long enough, Noah would take her back inside where she was safe. Perhaps he would send Davey out instead. But Noah did not move. He looked from Dovey to the clouds above, and she knew that he was praying. She knew he was listening to their creator.

Perhaps Dovey should do the same. She turned her attention towards the creator, to the one who had preserved her life, who had called her into the boat to begin with. As soon as Dovey looked at him, he spoke to her.

'Go,' he simply said.

That was that then. Without another moment of hesitation, Dovey flew off, leaving Noah's outstretched hand behind her.

Noah whooped and cheered as Dovey took off on the wind, flying higher and higher, off to search for a sign of life. If the creator wanted her out here, where the waters seemed to go on forever, then she would trust him with her life because he'd given it to her. Yes, she would do whatever he asked of her.

*He also released a dove to see if the water had receded and it could find dry ground. But the dove could find no place to land because the water still covered the ground. So it returned to the boat, and Noah held out his hand and drew the dove back inside. After waiting another seven days, Noah released the dove again. This time the dove returned to him in the evening with a fresh olive leaf in its beak. Then Noah knew that the floodwaters were almost gone.* (Genesis 8:8–11)

But how will we be saved?


*If you openly declare that Jesus is Lord and believe in your heart that God raised him from the dead, you will be saved. For it is by believing in your heart that you are made right with God, and it is by openly declaring your faith that you are saved. (Romans 10:9–10)*

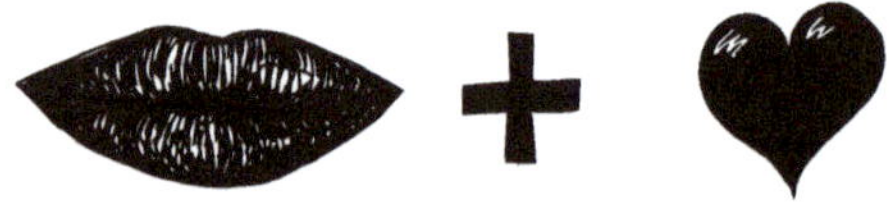

# Tallow

Tallow sat beside the Jordan River, his crossed legs beneath him, watching the glistening water before him. The river was full, almost overflowing its banks, and the town of Adam hustled and bustled behind him. Tallow needed to think, and the river had always been good for that.

Today the sun shone bright, but Tallow barely noticed its warmth. He was all alone by the river this morning, which was good, because nobody was here to see him cry. Tallow was twelve years old, but he carried a heavy load, and the last thing he needed was for any of the other children to see him crying.

Tallow's Mama was sick. They hadn't told Tallow or the other children yet … so he couldn't be sure, but it was clear to Tallow that something was seriously wrong. Mama was pale and had lost weight. She stayed in bed most days now. She tried to smile for Tallow  whenever he entered her room, but it wasn't enough. Tallow could see past her smiles.

Her eyes were hollow and dull, and the worst part was that Tallow could tell Mama was afraid. She tried to hide the fear in her eyes, but he knew Mama too well. He could see it.

His eyes filled with tears now at the thought of her, and he brushed a runaway tear from his cheek with the back of his fist. He wished they would be honest with him, that she and Papa would just tell him straight. After all, Tallow was twelve years old. He wasn't a baby.

He shoved his hands into his pockets as he watched the surface of the water. His fingers grazed against something. What was that? Tallow wrapped his fingers around the contents of his pocket and remembered he hadn't finished the pistachios from yesterday. He was thankful for them now. He pulled out the nuts and popped one in his mouth and then another and another.

Tallow was about to eat the last pistachio when suddenly something happened in the water before him. Tallow paused and furrowed his brow. Was the water changing direction? But how? The water churned and swirled and looked nothing like it had only moments earlier.

Tallow froze, his mouth still open, and the pistachio in his fingertips. He blinked unbelieving eyes as he watched the bubbling water. Something odd was happening in the river, right where Tallow sat. He jumped to his feet and watched as the water seemed to … stop flowing, as though something mighty held the water back, as though the water was hitting an invisible force.

More water flowed towards where Tallow stood. The more water that flowed, the higher the wall of water grew before him. The pistachio dropped from Tallow's fingertips, bouncing off his shoe and plopping into the river, where it was drawn up into the water wall.

What was this? What was going on here? Were Tallow's eyes deceiving him?

Tallow strained his eyes, scanning up and down the river, back and forth, as far as he could see, but there was nothing. How could this be? What was holding back the river, and how could anything be powerful enough to do so?

Tallow needed to run into town. He needed to find an adult, someone who might be able to explain what was going on here. After all, there had to be a reasonable explanation. There had to be.

As Tallow turned on his heel and bounded back up towards town, heading for home, he couldn't help but wonder if the ceasing of the river's flow would not be easily explained away … if, perhaps, Tallow had witnessed a miracle.

'Papa,' Tallow called out as he raced through their front door. But Papa's work belt was gone. Of course he would be working.

'Is that you, Tallow?' Mama called from her bedroom. Tallow's heart sank, and he slowed as he approached her room.

'I'm sorry if I woke you,' he whispered as he stepped through the door. It was dark inside, and it took a moment for his eyes to adjust. He shouldn't bother Mama. He should have thought before calling out so loudly.

'What is it, Tallow?' Mama asked. 'You sounded excited.' She reached for his hand. As she took his hand into hers, his emotions welled up inside of him again, surprising him. He wanted to jump onto her bed and into her arms. He missed Mama so much.

'What is it, Tallow?' she asked again, and he knew she was worried now. Should he tell her? Probably not … but the news of the strange event bubbled up inside him and he knew how much she would love to hear. He missed sharing his world with her.

As Tallow relayed what he had seen beside the river, excitement rose within him, and the sparkle returned to Mama's eyes. Oh, how he had missed her sparkly eyes. He blinked back tears as she slowly rose from the bed and reached for her coat.

What was she doing? Surely she wasn't coming to the river with him? Was that a good idea? But there was no stopping

Mama now. Tallow hadn't seen her move this fast for many months. Perhaps this was exactly what Mama needed … to see a miracle.

He followed her out the front door, and they headed down to the river, hand in hand.

*Look, the Ark of the Covenant, which belongs to the Lord of the whole earth, will lead you across the Jordan River!*

*The priests will carry the Ark of the Lord, the Lord of all the earth. As soon as their feet touch the water, the flow of water will be cut off upstream, and the river will stand up like a wall.*

*So the people left their camp to cross the Jordan, and the priests who were carrying the Ark of the Covenant went ahead of them. It was the harvest season, and the Jordan was overflowing its banks. But as soon as the feet of the priests who were carrying the Ark touched the water at the river's edge, the water above that point began backing up a great distance away at a town called Adam, which is near Zarethan. And the water below that point flowed on to the Dead Sea until the riverbed was dry. Then all the people crossed over near the town of Jericho.* (Joshua 3:11,13–16)

# Arly

Arly stepped into the kitchen. It was only just light enough to see. As usual, she was the first one awake, though it wouldn't be long until the children woke. Arly smiled to herself as her gaze swept over her kitchen.

Arly was content. It was an unusual feeling, but one that she was slowly becoming accustomed to. For the first time in her young life, she had a home. Her own kitchen, even. Stability.

The Israelites had crossed the Jordan River and taken possession of Jerusalem only a few months ago, but Arly's community had thrived from the day their feet first hit the soil. And Arly knew that as long as they remained close to Him, as long as they followed their God, things would continue to go well for them.

Tears filled her eyes, as they so often did now. 'Thank you,' she whispered to him.

The fruit bowl on her kitchen counter caught her eye. Her brow furrowed. Was she seeing clearly? Daylight approached with each passing minute, and she could already see more clearly than when she'd first stepped into the kitchen. But Arly could have sworn there was more fruit this morning than there had been last night.

Had Koda added to the bowl once Arly was in bed? No. He'd been asleep before she'd even gone to bed. How odd. Her stomach rumbled. She reached for an apple and twirled it in her hand, marvelling at its size and its colour.

Arly salivated as she took her chopping knife and positioned her breadboard on the bench, preparing to chop her apple in half.

She paused for a moment, eyeing the board. She moved her apple and knife to the side and flipped over the breadboard, puzzled. Where was the stain? Arly had cut black radishes for dinner last night, and they had left a terrible stain on her breadboard.

But this morning, the stain was gone. But how? Had Koda scrubbed it for her during the night? Of course he hadn't! She laughed at the thought. Arly turned the board over again, back and forth, searching for any sign of the radish stain, but there was none.

*You will experience all these blessings if you obey*
*the Lord your God:*
*Your towns and your fields will be blessed.*
*Your children and your crops will be blessed.*
*The offspring of your herds and flocks will be blessed.*
*Your fruit baskets and breadboards will be blessed.*
*Wherever you go and whatever you do, you will be blessed.*
(Deuteronomy 28:2–6)

Is it true, that you have my name written on your hand? Then my joy has no words.

*Yet Jerusalem says, 'The Lord has deserted us; the Lord has forgotten us.'*
*'Never! Can a mother forget her nursing child? Can she feel no love for the child she has borne? But even if that were possible, I would never forget you! See, I have written your name on the palms of my hands.' (Isaiah 49:14-16)*

# Guilt

God had forgiven David for what happened with Bathsheba many years ago, but sometimes David still thought of it. If David was feeling low, or if he was especially tired, then the guilt would creep back in. David never spoke of it. Not out loud. Not to anyone. Nobody knew of the guilt that followed him around, nobody except for his God.

On a deeper level, David knew he could trust God; he knew God had forgiven him, so why did his guilt still remain?

This was why hearing Nathan's words today had sent tears streaming down David's face. Nathan heard directly from the living God, from David's God, so David knew Nathan's words could be trusted. Even still, they were hard to believe.

Nathan said God had chosen Solomon—David's son with Bathsheba—to be the next king. Chosen Solomon even though David had taken Bathsheba for himself, even though he had organised Uriah, her husband, to be put to death, even though David had many other sons to his many other wives.

Was it true?

David remembered the words he had written to God after having Uriah killed.

*Have mercy on me God, because of your unfailing love for me. O God, because of your goodness and your compassion, please blot out the stain caused by my sins. I can see my rebellion, I can't escape it Lord, my rebellion haunts me.*

David was alone in his bedroom now, so he fell to the floor and lay face down to worship God. David had no words. It was too much. God was kind to him. Today, God had made it crystal clear that he forgave David. Though no one else knew of David's guilt, God knew, and David was truly forgiven.

*Yet the Lord, the God of Israel, has chosen me from among all my father's family to be king over Israel forever. For he has chosen the tribe of Judah to rule, and from among the families of Judah he chose my father's family. And from among my father's sons the Lord was pleased to make me king over all Israel. And from among my sons – for the Lord has given me many – he chose Solomon to succeed me on the throne of Israel and to rule over the Lord's kingdom.* (1 Chronicles 28:4–5)

Let my thoughts align with yours.


*May the words of my mouth
and the meditation of my heart
be pleasing to you,
O Lord, my rock and my redeemer.*
(Psalm 19:14)

# Maai

Maai stood at her kitchen bench, staring out at the dirt road. There was mouldy bread on the counter beside her that she hadn't bothered to throw out yet. She needed to clean the dishes and collect some water too, other tasks she had managed to put off so far this morning. She watched her husband out on the road, talking with a small group of men from Gibeon.

The entire town of Gibeon was in a state of unrest as of late, fearful of the Israelites and their all-powerful God. Everybody had heard the stories of how the God of the Israelites had freed his people from captivity in Egypt, and he hadn't stopped there. It seemed the God of the Israelites had given much of the land surrounding Gibeon to his people. The people of Gibeon feared their town would be next. Would the Israelite God gift their town to his people as well?

The men on the road looked to be up to something, and Maai was curious. With one last look at the mouldy bread and piled-up dishes, she wiped her hands on a dishcloth and went out to join them. She would clean up later.

Maai was surprised when she came closer to discover that their neighbour, Zoref, was dressed entirely in rags. Nothing like his usual attire. Zoref was sitting atop a donkey with a weathered saddlebag. Zoref's sandals were worn out and patchy, and he carried old, patched wineskins.

What was going on?

'It's not enough.' Maai's husband, Carmi, shook his head. He noticed Maai then and she opened her mouth to question, but he beat her to it.

'We're sending Zoref to the Israelites,' he told her.

Maai felt the blood rush from her face. That did not sound like a good idea.

'But why?' was all she could muster.

Carmi's eyes were alight with nervous excitement as he turned to explain.

'We'll pretend we are from a faraway land. We'll ask the Israelite people to make a peace treaty with us. We will make them take an oath to swear that they will not harm us.'

Maai could not believe what she heard. Had they lost their minds? She knew the townspeople were afraid, but this would never work. Words escaped her as she looked from Carmi to Zoref.

'We must convince them we have been travelling for many months. We must make it believable. Our lives depend on it.'

Just a moment. While Carmi had said Zoref would visit the Israelites, he was now using the word 'we'. But she had known as soon as he'd explained their plan to her. He would not send Zoref alone. Her husband may have been crazy, but he was also brave.

'Mouldy bread.' Carmi pointed a finger into the air. 'We need mouldy bread to make it believable.'

*But when the people of Gibeon heard what Joshua had done to Jericho and Ai, they resorted to deception to save themselves. They sent ambassadors to Joshua, loading their donkeys with weathered saddlebags and old, patched wineskins. They put on worn-out, patched sandals and ragged clothes. And the bread they took with them was dry and mouldy. When they arrived at the camp of Israel at Gilgal, they told Joshua and the men of Israel, 'We have come from a distant land to ask you to make a peace treaty with us.' (Joshua 9:3–6)*

# Compassion

Matthew was annoyed. There were too many people here. They were everywhere, and he was peopled out! All Matthew wanted was some space and some quiet. Every single screech and every single holler irritated him now. He tried not to show it on his face, but he wanted them all to go away.

Surely the others were feeling overwhelmed too?

There were just too many people. Matthew looked to Jesus. Matthew was sure he would find at least a hint of frustration on his face. But the expression on Jesus's face was anything but frustrated. Matthew studied the way Jesus watched the people and the word settled over him.

Compassion. It was compassion.

*When he saw the crowds, he had compassion on them because they were confused and helpless, like sheep without a shepherd. He said to his disciples, 'The harvest is great, but the workers are few. So pray to the Lord who is in charge of the harvest; ask him to send more workers into his fields.'* (Matthew 9:36–38)

# Romee

Romee was a stone who lived on the riverbed in the depths of the River Jordan. Romee was large and grey and had never ever moved. Throughout his many years beneath the river's waters, Romee had been knocked and bumped by smaller rocks that passed him by. Because of this, Romee had slowly changed shape and become somewhat rounder than he once was. His jagged edges had been smoothed over.

Romee watched the smaller rocks as they journeyed across the Jordan, and he wondered what it felt like to move.

But Romee had an important job. He was only a rock … but there was life that lived beneath him. Romee was home to a great number of algae, plants, and even little fish who hid and spawned tucked in at his side. Yes, Romee had an important job. But even so, as the years went by, Romee found himself wondering about whether there might be more to his life. If there might be more to see.

Every day, he watched the smaller rocks as they passed him by. Every day, he watched the little fish as they came, and they went, as they swam higher and higher until out of view. Where did they go? What did they see? Romee would have asked the fish, but he was a rock. Besides sheltering beneath him, the fish paid Romee no attention. After all, they were busy, and Romee understood.

But Romee only became more curious with time. His questions grew louder. Was Romee missing out on something?

Was there more to see than his life beneath the sea had offered him?

One day, Romee directed his thoughtful longings towards the creator. Without using words, Romee told the creator how he longed to see where the fish went each day and how he wondered about what it was like to move like the small stones that travelled by him. As Romee shared his thoughts with the creator, he realised something in the sharing alone seemed to ease his frustration. He wondered why he had never thought to share with the creator before. Though the creator was silent, Romee sensed he had been heard. From that day on, Romee spoke to the creator about his wonderings. Romee spoke to him every day.

Today was no different. The river was full and wild, and Romee watched as a smaller rock rushed on by. As the familiar longing took hold, Romee turned straight to his creator.

'Where is the rock going?' his heart whispered, a question he had asked many times now. 'What does it feel like to be tossed to and fro? Is it scary to move, or is it wonderful? What will the little rock see today?' Romee was quiet for a minute or so. 'I long to feel it,' he added. 'I long to see something new.'

Then Romee sat still, because that was all he was able to do. But there it was again. A feeling Romee was becoming accustomed to. A peace. It seemed there was something about handing his wonderings over to the creator that left Romee feeling content. Though nothing had changed for Romee and his situation remained the same, Romee felt heard. It was an odd transaction that didn't make sense, but it was good.

And today, when Romee was full to the brim with peace from the creator, something new did happen.

Romee heard a whisper.

*Gilgal.*

It was just one simple word, but it was as clear as if Romee had spoken it himself. What was a Gilgal? Romee had never heard of it before. Had the creator spoken so clearly to Romee, and taught him a brand-new word? But why? Before Romee had a chance to think on it, the water around him began to stir up. It became fast and was wilder than Romee had ever seen the waters of the Jordan. It churned and bubbled, and the water around Romee became murky, which made it hard to see. Many smaller rocks crashed into Romee as they were tossed to and fro, and the fish disappeared, hidden from sight.

*Gilgal.*

There it was again! What was a Gilgal? What was the creator trying to tell him? Romee had no idea, but he watched as the water churned all around him.

And then it happened.

The water level around Romee lowered. It became lower and lower until it had completely disappeared. All of a sudden, for the first time in Romee's life, he no longer sat beneath the water, because the water was gone.

The sun was brilliant and bright. It hit Romee square on his surface, and he instantly felt its warmth. Romee couldn't believe it. Was this a dream? Romee struggled to keep up with the changes around him.

Then he was trodden on by a foot. It was fast and over in an instant, but then another foot trod on his surface, then another and another. Romee watched as people passed over him, through the Jordan, walking on dry ground.

The people looked nothing like fish. They were something brand new. Romee's wildest dreams were coming true, and he felt the creator nearby. Romee might have cried, but he was a rock, so instead he did nothing. He watched and he waited to see what would happen next. Would the water return? Would he once again be submerged beneath the river? He took in every detail of his surroundings, of the people, of the sun.

Romee would never forget this day.

When the people had crossed the Jordan, some men remained on the riverbed, standing close beside where Romee sat. The men held a beautiful, large box up over their heads. It must have been heavy. What did it hold? Romee could tell the creator was nearby, but was he closer than Romee had imagined? Was the creator inside the beautiful box?

Romee turned his attention from the beautiful box to a group of men who were coming back down into the Jordan. They stopped close by where Romee sat. The men wandered back and forth with their heads down. Were they inspecting the rocks?

A man with dark hair and bushy eyebrows knelt beside Romee. The man looked Romee over and brushed his hands over Romee's surface. With a nod of his head, the man wrapped his giant arms around Romee and heaved him up from where he sat. From where he had always sat.

It was the moment Romee moved for the first time in his life. It was a moment Romee had dreamed of for many years, and though his head was spinning, he had been right about moving! It was wonderful.

Romee was carried on the large man's shoulder up out of the Jordan to a dry, clear space, where he was plonked down onto the ground in a new place. A place named Gilgal. Romee could hardly believe his luck as he took in his surroundings. He now sat beside grass and trees, beside birds and people.

Romee recalled his deep longings, his wonderings and the way he had shared them with the creator. As he sat in his new home, surrounded by so many wonderful new things, Romee was sure about one thing.

He had been heard.

But not only had he been heard, the creator cared for the deep longings of Romee's heart.

*When all the people had crossed the Jordan, the Lord said to Joshua, "Now choose twelve men, one from each tribe. Tell them, 'Take twelve stones from the very place where the priests are standing in the middle of the Jordan. Carry them out and pile them up at the place where you will camp tonight.'"*

*So Joshua called together the twelve men he had chosen—one from each of the tribes of Israel. He told them, "Go into the middle of the Jordan, in front of the Ark of the Lord your God. Each of you must pick up one stone and carry it out on your shoulder—twelve stones in all, one for each of the twelve tribes of Israel. We will use these stones to build a memorial. In the future your children will ask you, 'What do these stones mean?' Then you can tell them, 'They remind us that the Jordan River stopped flowing when the Ark of the Lord's Covenant went across.' These stones will stand as a memorial among the people of Israel forever."*

*The people crossed the Jordan on the tenth day of the first month. Then they camped at Gilgal, just east of Jericho. It was there at Gilgal that Joshua piled up the twelve stones taken from the Jordan River. (Joshua 4:1–7,19–20)*

# Joey

Joey was an encourager. It was his gift. It wasn't something he tried to do, but something that came naturally to him. He remembered, as a young child, watching his mama's face as she tried to keep up with the other women in the kitchen. Joey's mama had not been good at cooking. But Joey had seen the discouragement in her eyes and had made it his mission from that day forward to compliment his mama on every meal she made him.

Joey loved to encourage people, and he had seen that same look of discouragement today in the eyes of one of the apostles. Joey had seen the man's discouraged look and had recognised a need he could fill. A way Joey could help. He knew exactly what he would do.

Joey walked quickly through his field now, his worn shoes tackling the overgrown grass at his feet. Joey had owned the field for many years, and today he would sell it. It wouldn't be difficult—the owner of the neighbouring property, an elderly man named Loty, had wanted to buy Joey's field for quite some time. Joey headed toward Loty's property now, where he hoped to come to an arrangement this very day.

Then Joey would take the money from the sale and give it all to the apostles. It was a generous thing to do, but he believed in what the apostles were doing. He wanted to get behind them. He wanted to encourage them, and not just with lip service.

This would do it. He was sure.

*For instance, there was Joseph, the one the apostles nick-named Barnabas (which means 'Son of Encouragement'). He was from the tribe of Levi and came from the island of Cyprus. He sold a field he owned and brought the money to the apostles. (Acts 4:36–37)*

What if you really do love me?
What if you really are for me?


*What shall we say about such wonderful things as these?*
*If God is for us, who can ever be against us?*
(Romans 8:31)

# Covered

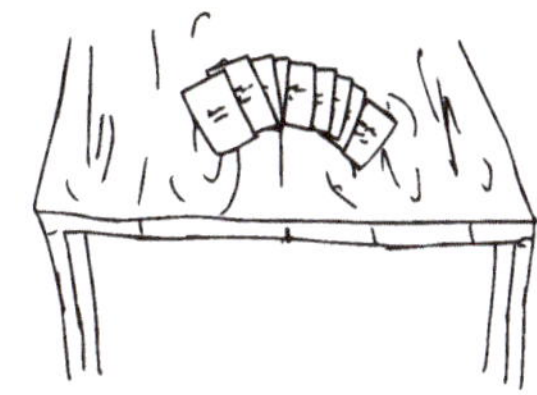

A wooden table was before him. He sat beside it, emptying his vessel of its contents. He used his hands to spread them out on the tabletop.

They were her sins. He had them all.

They were her secret sins. Sins she carried around with her like a heavy blanket of guilt. They were hurting her, their weight slowing her down, and now they were seen by his eyes alone.

What would he do with them now that he saw them?

How would he deal with her sins?

He passed his eyes over each and every one until he had seen them all.

He rose from his chair and stretched out his arms, and he covered her sins with himself.

*You spread out our sins before you—our secret sins—*
*and you see them all.*
(Psalm 90:8)

*You forgave the guilt of your people—*
*yes, you covered all their sins.*
(Psalm 85:2)

# Mount Zion

The city sat on top of a tall mountain. It wasn't just any mountain, but a holy mountain. The city was so high and so magnificent that every person on earth rejoiced to see it. Even those people who didn't know who the city belonged to rejoiced. Everything that had breath rejoiced to see the city. They called out, hollering and cheering, using any sound that they could muster.

Because he lived there.

'It is Mount Zion,' his people called out.

*How great is the Lord, how deserving of praise,*
*in the city of God, which sits on his holy mountain!*
*It is high and magnificent;*
*the whole earth rejoices to see it!*
*Mount Zion, the holy mountain,*
*is the city of the great King!*
(Psalm 48:1–2)

# Dixie

'Do I matter to you?' Dixie asked him.

He opened the large book that lay on his table and flicked through the pages by memory. He smiled just slightly when he came to the page he'd been looking for.

He swivelled the book around so it faced her and, without any words, used his large finger to point to the top of the page.

Intrigued, Dixie stepped forward. What could it be? She had no idea, but she read aloud.

'Dixie woke up earlier than usual this morning.'

It was her name written there, in his book! Her eyes shot up to meet his. There was a twinkle in his eye as he redirected her back to the page. Dixie didn't understand. Were the words here written about her? Surely not.

Dixie placed a finger beneath the line and read on.

'Dixie lay in bed for twenty minutes before slipping on her robe and slippers. She went downstairs to let Mickey out of his cage.'

Tears sprang to Dixie's eyes. The words were about her.

She remembered Mickey and how much she'd loved him. Mickey had been more than a pet to her. He'd been her best friend. The words were blurry now. She blinked away her tears and read on, eager to hear what happened next.

'Dixie sat in her favourite chair and stared out the window at the yard, watching Mickey run around for ten minutes.'

Dixie laughed. She had loved to watch Mickey play. But

she shook her head. Had he watched her so intently? Had he loved to watch her as she loved to watch Mickey?

She hadn't known.

Dixie was speechless. She wiped a runaway tear from her cheek and read on, her voice cracking with emotion.

'Dixie switched on her jug, prepared her coffee, and was adding the boiling water when there was a knock at her front door. Dixie jumped a little, wondering who could be visiting so early. She worried because she hadn't brushed her teeth, so she glanced in the living room mirror before unlocking and opening the front door. It was Marly, Dixie's neighbour, and Marly was crying.'

Dixie stopped reading. She remembered that day. It had been many, many years ago, and Marly had fought with her husband. Marly had come in and stayed for a while, the two having coffee and eventually breakfast together while they talked it through.

It was clear to Dixie now. He had recorded a day from her life. The realisation settled over her and took her breath away. But how could it be, and why would he bother? She eyeballed the book. It was large both in height and depth. Were there more days recorded here?

Even as the question formed in her mind, his Spirit wrapped around her, whispering in a voice only she would understand. He replied to her with his own question.

'Do you matter to me?'


*You saw me before I was born.*
*Every day of my life was recorded in your book.*
*Every moment was laid out before a single day had passed.*
(Psalm 139:16)

You give hope, even when the world screams
hopelessness.


*The Lord is my strength and shield.*
*I trust him with all my heart.*
*He helps me, and my heart is filled with joy.*
*I burst out in songs of thanksgiving.*
(Psalm 28:7)

# Zalmu

It was true Zalmu had joined the group of believers. He'd been sharing their meals and living in their community, and he was enjoying himself here.

But Zalmu was not like the others.

Zalmu had heard their stories about Jesus and about why they had founded their community, but he wasn't buying it. Zalmu hadn't experienced Jesus with his own eyes, and as much as he wanted to be a part of it all, he just couldn't bring himself to believe. The people assumed he was like them, a believer. Zalmu knew he should probably just leave, but he was enjoying himself too much and the people were kind. They were generous, too. And it wasn't just the atmosphere. Zalmu had spotted a beautiful girl in the camp.

No, Zalmu wasn't ready to leave. Not yet.

He stood now in the eating quarters. The people were gathered and were listening to two of the disciples—Peter and John. They had just returned from prison, and Zalmu was surprised to see them back. They had been jailed for apparently healing a lame man using the name of Jesus. Zalmu hadn't been there that day, so was again hearing things second-hand.

'Our captors commanded that we never speak again in the name of Jesus,' Peter said loudly so the whole crowd could hear.

The people around Zalmu gasped and shook their heads, but Zalmu just listened.

'So we told them we would listen to God and not to them.'

Zalmu was sceptical. Their speech was brave, but how were the disciples released after saying something like that?

Zalmu felt a shift in the people around him. They began to pray; an outcry of praise rose into the air as they lifted their hands to the heavens. Were they thanking God for releasing the disciples?

'O Lord, creator of heaven and earth, the sea, and everything in them.' Peter prayed out loud, and a shiver ran up Zalmu's spine.

'You spoke long ago by the Holy Spirit through our ancestor, David. David asked why the nations were so angry. Why they wasted their time with futile plans? The kings of the earth prepared for battle, and the rulers gathered against the Lord and his Messiah.'

It was clear that Peter was remembering King David's words. Then Peter's eyes flung open as though recognising their meaning for the first time.

'In fact, this is exactly what has happened here today, there were so many in this very city united against Jesus, whom you anointed. But everything that they did was determined beforehand by you, God.'

Now Zalmu was confused. Were King David's words written about this very time, right here and right now?

Suddenly, Peter dropped to his knees and John kneeled beside him.

'And now, O Lord.' Peter's voice had changed, and Zalmu stretched taller to see him more clearly. Peter was silent for a moment, regaining his composure. 'Hear their threats, and give us, your servants, great boldness in preaching your word.' His voice broke, full of raw emotion, and Zalmu found his eyesight had become blurry.

Something like scales seemed to fall from his eyes as he watched the men, and his tears overflowed and ran down his cheeks.

'Stretch out your hand with healing power,' Peter continued. 'May miraculous signs and wonders be done through the name of Jesus.'

There was something happening around Zalmu. It was as though the people were no longer alone here. There was a presence beside him, an almost tangible presence.

And that was when Zalmu realised he believed.

*As soon as they were freed, Peter and John returned to the other believers and told them what the leading priests and elders had said. When they heard the report, all the believers lifted their voices together in prayer to God.*

*'And now, O Lord, hear their threats, and give us, your servants, great boldness in preaching your word.'*

*After this prayer, the meeting place shook, and they were all filled with the Holy Spirit. Then they preached the word of God with boldness. (Acts 4:23–24,29,31)*

Can you please help me, right where I am, to reach the place right where you are?


*In those days when you pray, I will listen. If you look for me wholeheartedly, you will find me. I will be found by you, says the Lord.* (Jeremiah 29:12–14)

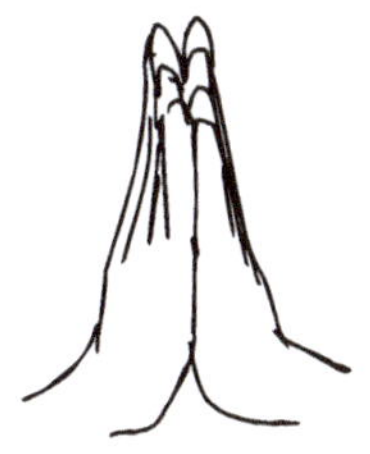

# A Breath

His mouth was slightly ajar, but he took in a deep breath through his nostrils. Drawing oxygen into his lungs, they were filled, right up to the brim. And then, just like that, in a matter of seconds, the air was released. Expelled out through parted lips. The breath was over. It was just one breath. A single breath. Over as quickly as it had begun.

*You have made my life no longer*
*than the width of my hand.*
*My entire lifetime is just a moment to you;*
*at best, each of us is but a breath.*
*We are merely moving shadows,*
*and all our busy rushing ends in nothing.*
*We heap up wealth,*
*not knowing who will spend it.*
*And so, Lord, where do I put my hope?*
*My only hope is in you.*
(Psalm 39:5–7)

# Meadow

It had been a kind thing to do. Meadow knew that. She would not have dinner herself tonight. Her stomach rumbled as she closed the door behind her, leaving the scent of freshly baked bread inside the Zulay home. The Zulay family were sick, and they were very poor. Meadow would be hungry, but she felt full in another way. She smiled to herself as she felt the Spirit near.

A vision flashed before her mind's eye. Meadow stopped in her tracks, halfway down the steps. The vision was so clear, it took her breath away. It was a vision of fine, pure white linen floating in a gentle breeze right before her face…

The vision faded as quickly as it had appeared, and Meadow knew it was a vision from him. But what did it mean? She held her breath, willing the vision to return, willing its meaning to be revealed.

But there was nothing.

Meadow continued on down the steps and out to the path where she pondered the vision of the floating linen all the way home.

*For the time has come for the wedding feast of the Lamb, and his bride has prepared herself. She has been given the finest of pure white linen to wear. For the fine linen represents the good deeds of God's holy people. (Revelation 19:7–8)*

# Checklist 

Joshua had been waiting for this moment. Now the Israelites had defeated the people of Ai, he wanted to be sure they followed all the instructions correctly, to ensure the people of Israel would be blessed. He had already built the altar using uncut stones, then copied the instructions onto the stones while the people watched, so that part was complete.

Now, Joshua held the instructions from Moses in his hand. Although he'd been preparing for this and had read them over many times, he would still check them off as they followed each one today. He took a deep breath, pushing his nerves aside, and scrolled his eyes over the first few sentences.

'We must split the people into two groups,' he announced to the leaders first, then called out louder to all those within earshot.

Joshua's words took off on the crowd. Before long, the people had divided themselves into two very large groups. One group stood directly in front of Mount Gerizim, and the other group stood in front of Mount Ebal.

Okay, everything was looking good so far.

Joshua scanned the group to his left, then the group to his right. He nodded and looked back down to the instructions. They could not be too careful. There was a lot riding on this, and he was desperate for them to get it right.

'Now the groups need to face each other,' he called out. His instructions were once again repeated through the crowd.

Starting with those closest, the people turned to face one another. Minutes passed by.

When Joshua next looked up, the entire sea of faces was looking to each other. He stood as tall as he was able to look over both groups, making sure that each and every person had obeyed and was facing the right way. Satisfied, he nodded before looking back down to his instructions.

There was anticipation in the air. The people were buzzing with excitement and Joshua was too, but he was determined to get things right. He pushed his excitement aside and zoned in on Moses's instructions, using every bit of concentration he could muster. He found the last sentence he had read and read on.

'Now the Levitical priests must walk between the two groups, and the priests must carry the Ark of the Lord's Covenant.'

This instruction sent a wave of excitement through the crowd. While their voices were hushed, Joshua could hear their shuffling feet and stifled whispers.

There was sobbing as the priests walked between the Israelites, and Joshua found his own eyes became moist too. It was the Ark of their Lord, after all, and the people loved him.

When the priests were in place, Joshua went back to his instructions. He felt their eyes on him as he read what they must do next. It was time. He cleared his throat.

'Now I will read to you every word that Moses has written in the Book of Instruction.'

The people fell silent. There was not a sound, no shuffling feet, or hushed whispers. Nobody wanted to miss a word. Joshua had their full attention.

*Then all the Israelites—foreigners and native-born alike—along with the elders, officers, and judges, were divided into two groups. One group stood in front of Mount Gerizim, the other in front of Mount Ebal. Each group faced the other, and between them stood the Levitical priests carrying the Ark of the Lord's Covenant. This was all done according to the commands that Moses, the servant of the Lord, had previously given for blessing the people of Israel.*

*Joshua then read to them all the blessings and curses Moses had written in the Book of Instruction. Every word of every command that Moses had ever given was read to the entire assembly of Israel, including the women and children and the foreigners who lived among them.* (Joshua 8:33–35)

# Poured Out

I am swimming in liquid love. If I reach out my arms,
they float beside me.
I am safe here. Your love holds me up.
I do not drown and no matter how far I swim away,
your love covers me.
Whether my feelings align with yours, your love covers me.
Even when I can't remember it, your love still covers me.
You always cover me.

*So we praise God for the glorious grace he has poured out
on us who belong to his dear Son.* (Ephesians 1:6)

# Elda

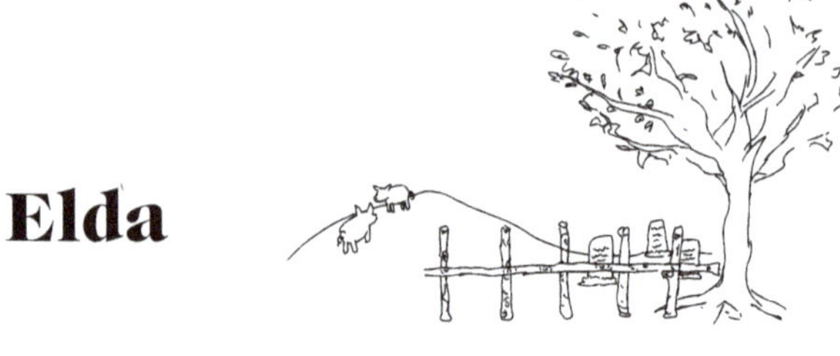

It had been three years to the day since Elda had lost her daughter. Lati had only been four years old when she died, and Elda's heart would never be whole again. In some ways, Elda felt she too had died that day. Many days, she wished she had.

Elda stood now, peering over the grassy fields before her, aching to be able to cross them, to visit Lati's grave. But this was as far as she could come. It had been so long now since Elda had been able to sit beside Lati's grave, to sit beside her resting place and feel close to her, to speak to her and tidy up her gravesite. Elda craved it more than anything else on earth. She fell asleep at night, imagining she was there, with Lati, and woke up in the morning yearning to be.

But two crazy men lived in the cemetery now. They had taken over the whole area and were so violent and so dangerous that no one else could visit. The gate was as far as Elda could come. Today, she would stay here. She would stay all day. She had packed a lunch and had enough water to last for hours, so she would stay. It had been three years today since losing Lati, so where else would she go?

Elda took off her coat and was searching for a soft patch of earth to spread it out on when she heard a sound. She fell to the ground, crouching down low and stayed completely still, listening, and watching through the gate.

There were footsteps.

Somebody was walking, a man. He crossed the fields and was heading towards the cemetery. Elda stood up to call out to the stranger, to warn him not to go that way. But her heart fell. It was too late. The stranger had already been spotted.

The two crazy men emerged from the shadows, looking wilder than ever, ready to defend their territory. They were a terrifying sight to behold—all wild hair and crazy eyes and clenched fists. Elda shuddered. To think her baby lived over there, beside them, sent panic rushing through her. It was something she rarely let herself think of.

The stranger was not deterred. He obviously had no idea of the danger before him. Should Elda run for help? He could be killed, and there was nothing she would be able to do. He would be attacked any moment now. She was sure of it. The stranger stood at a distance from the two men, and they seemed to be talking.

Elda was surprised. If only she could make out what they were saying. Though running for help was a good idea, her feet remained glued to the ground. Instead, she watched from behind the gate.

After a minute or so of conversation, none of which Elda had been able to make out, the two crazy men and the stranger turned to face the hillside. What were they looking at? There was nothing there except a herd of pigs.

Were they looking at the pigs? The thought had barely entered Elda's mind when the pigs took off running without warning. They took off with such urgency that Elda jumped with fright at their departure. The pigs seemed united in their direction, bolting towards the cliff's edge. Elda watched, barely believing her eyes as the pigs jumped from the cliff, each and every one of them, tumbling to their deaths.

What was happening here? This made no sense.

Turning her attention back to the men on the field, she saw that the two crazy men had fallen to their knees. The stranger closed the distance between them with large strides, then kneeled beside the men. He held an arm around each of their shoulders, and his head hung low between them.

What was he saying to the crazy men? And, more importantly, why were they silent and still and not violently thumping the stranger? Elda had no idea.

The stranger looked up and turned his head then, looking back to Elda. Did he know Elda was there? Did he know she hid behind the gate? Surely not. That was impossible. Though they were a fair distance apart, Elda had the feeling that the stranger could see her. He implored her with his eyes, *'Go to Lati's grave.'*

*When Jesus arrived on the other side of the lake, in the region of the Gaderenes, two men who were possessed by demons met him. They came out of the tombs and were so violent that no one could go through that area.*

*There happened to be a large herd of pigs feeding in the distance. So the demons begged, 'If you cast us out, send us into that herd of pigs.'*

*'All right, go!' Jesus commanded them. So the demons came out of the men and entered the pigs, and the whole herd plunged down the steep hillside into the lake and drowned in the water.* (Matthew 8:28,30–32)

# Example

'But why me? Why did you choose me to help build your kingdom, to help write your book? Why did you choose me when I attacked your people, and I even killed them?' Paul asked.

'So others would know that their sins, even their worst sins, could be forgiven too,' God replied.

*This is a trustworthy saying, and everyone should accept it: 'Christ Jesus came into the world to save sinners'—and I am the worst of them all. But God had mercy on me so that Christ Jesus could use me as a prime example of his great patience with even the worst sinners. Then others will realise that they, too, can believe in him and receive eternal life. (1 Timothy 1:15–16)*

# Snake Trick

Aaron appeared out of nowhere, far out in the wilderness, beside the mountain of God. How had he known to come? Moses was still trembling when he embraced his brother. Still trembling and still in shock.

'Is everything okay?' Aaron pulled back from him, holding Moses by the shoulders. 'You look like you've seen a ghost.'

'He was here.' Moses pointed to a bush. 'He was here and he was speaking to me. And there was fire.' Moses was making no sense. Aaron looked from the bush back to Moses and raised his eyebrows just slightly, but he was concerned. He'd never seen Moses like this before.

"It was God, Aaron! It was the God of Israel,' Moses exclaimed, his eyes ablaze with raw emotion. 'God told me that I … that we … you and I, must rescue his people from slavery.'

Now Aaron's mouth hung open, and he was quite sure that Moses was losing his mind.

'Watch this.' Moses was so excited, he pushed Aaron back with his hand on Aaron's chest, then threw his wooden staff to the ground. Moses was acting like a madman. But as Aaron watched, his staff crashed into the dust, then suddenly transformed into a snake, right before his eyes.

Aaron jumped back, bewildered and stunned. What had been a staff just moments earlier was now alive. A living snake, slithering through the dust towards them.

Moses grinned. He looked back and forth between Aaron and the snake before kneeling down beside it. He reached out his hand to grab it by the tail.

'Be careful.' Aaron found his voice and stepped forward. Moses grasped the snake by the tail, and instantly it was transformed back into a staff.

*Now the Lord had said to Aaron, 'Go out into the wilderness to meet Moses.' So Aaron went and met Moses at the mountain of God, and he embraced him. Moses then told Aaron everything the Lord had commanded him to say. And he told him about the miraculous signs the Lord had commanded him to perform.* (Exodus 4:27–28)

# Stop Sun

'We need help,' the Gibeonites pleaded with the Israelites. 'The four kings under Adoni-zedek have combined forces against us, and we will surely be killed.'

'We will come,' Joshua, the leader of the Israelites replied as he gathered his forces and set out immediately for Gibeon.

'Do not be afraid,' the Lord whispered to Joshua. 'For I am with you and I will give you victory over them.'

So Joshua listened to his God and believed Him. The Israelites attacked the five kings and their great armies in defence of Gibeon on that very day. But as the battle ensued, daylight was running out. They would soon be fighting in the dark of the night.

'Would you let the sun stand still over Gibeon,' Joshua called out to the Lord, 'and would the moon stand still over the valley?' It was a big prayer, a giant prayer. But Joshua believed in the One who had created the heavens and the earth. Joshua believed God could do whatever he wanted.

The Lord loved that Joshua trusted in him. He loved that Joshua believed, so the Lord turned to the sun. 'Stay there,' the Lord said to the sun. 'Stop moving,' he told the moon.

And, for the first time since the creation of the sun, it stood still. And, for the first time since the hanging of the moon, it ceased to move.

The sky stayed still until the Israelites had conquered their enemies, until the people of Gibeon were safe from harm.

*So the sun stayed still and the moon stayed in place until the nation of Israel had defeated its enemies.*

*Is this event not recorded in the Book of Jashar? The sun stayed in the middle of the sky, and it did not set as on a normal day. There has never been a day like this one before or since, when the Lord answered such a prayer. Surely the Lord fought for Israel that day!* (Joshua 10:13–14)

# Home

There is a home for me. When I step inside, I am complete. The air is fresh here, the ventilation flawless. I can breathe inside these walls, and I fit here. This home welcomes me, always welcomes me, and I belong inside.

There's a space in the wall for a fridge and my fridge fits into it perfectly. All the kitchen towels are pink—my favourite colour—and the daisies on the table are my favourite flower. This home sees my details and cares about them!

There is not one place I would rather be than in this home. It whispers to me, even treasures me. It tells me I belong here. I don't need a key for my front door. My palm print is enough to allow me entry.

This home knows me—it reads me like a book; it sees me clearer than I see myself. A place where I truly belong.

*Lord, through all the generations,*
*you have been our home!*
(Psalm 90:1)

# Isbe

Isbe the deer was dying of thirst. She had never been thirsty like this before. Her thirst was so pervading that she thought of nothing else now. The other parts of life that usually pulled her attention this way and that had faded into the background.

There was only her need for water.

Isbe lay, her hind legs crumpled beneath her and her front hooves beside her face. It was where she had fallen, and she hadn't been able to move since. Her breathing had changed, and her mouth was so dry she could no longer swallow. Isbe slipped in and out of consciousness. She didn't cry out any more.

There was nothing that could help her now, only water. She thought of nothing else. Streams of water rushed through her mind's eye. She remembered the streams she had known. How she yearned for their waters now, how she longed for them. There was nothing else she needed. Nothing else.

Isbe was slipping away again, her consciousness melting into the air. As the darkness surrounded her, strong arms lifted her fragile frame from the ground.

When Isbe regained consciousness, she found herself in a new place. There were golden streams of water to her left and golden streams of water to her right. Renewed hope coursed through her veins, and she plunged her face into the stream beside her. She let the water rush into her open mouth. It washed through her nostrils and over her closed eyelids.

She was alive and she was free. The streams she had longed for filled every part of her. She was saved. She was satisfied.

*As the deer longs for streams of water,*
*so I long for you, O God.*
*I thirst for God, the living God.*
*When can I go and stand before him?*
(Psalm 42:1–2)

# Bloom

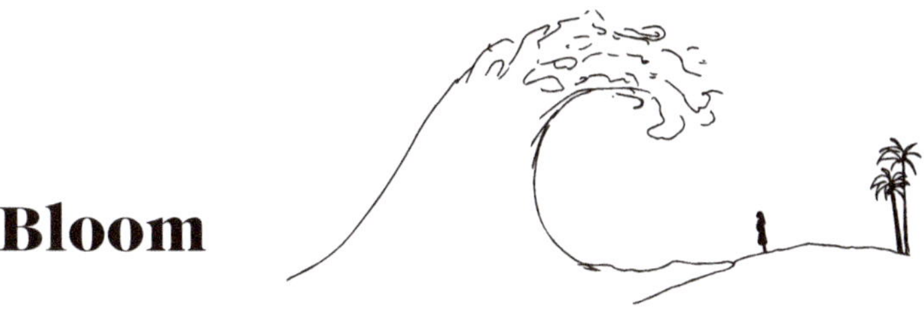

Bloom stood on the beach. The wind howled through her hair and the salt water sprayed against her cheeks as she watched the wild waves.

There had been a warning to stay off the beach today, but Bloom had to see for herself. The beach was deserted, and now she saw the roaring ocean, she understood why. Bloom had never seen the breakers this big. She watched as another wave crashed to the shore, its body so mighty, it sent a shiver down her spine. If she had been swimming beneath the giant wave, she would surely have perished.

The waves were so loud that Bloom had heard them from her home. Was the earth shaking beneath her feet with each mighty crash? The sand made it hard to tell. She stretched her head right back, breathing in the stormy sky, then let her eyes wander down the beach from her left to her right and back out to sea again. It was all so very big, so wild and alive!

Bloom felt very small.

*But mightier than the violent raging of the seas,*
*mightier than the breakers on the shore—*
*the Lord above is mightier than these!*
(Psalm 93:4)

# Heart Likeness

God was constructing a body for David. God smiled to himself as he placed the pieces together to form David, because God knew how big his life would be. David would be a king. Through David's line, God's Son would be born. God decided on David's features and his blood type, then he moved on to build David a heart. He paused for a moment, thinking about David's heart…

'I'll make it like mine,' he said to himself. Confirming it with a nod of his head, he created David's heart.

*But God removed Saul and replaced him with David, a man about whom God said, 'I have found David, son of Jesse, a man after my own heart. He will do everything I want him to do.' (Acts 13:22)*

Let me remember my first love—that it was you.


*This is what the Lord says:*
*'I remember how eager you were to please me as a young*
*bride long ago, how you loved me and followed me even*
*through the barren wilderness.'*
(Jeremiah 2:2)

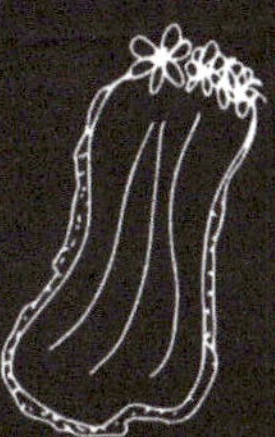

# Three

He sat in the belly of a giant fish. It was very dark and very warm and the fishy odour was overwhelming. But he was alive. Somehow. He had not obeyed the giver of life, a decision he now regretted with every fibre of his being. He would surely die inside this fish. What a way to go. For three days and three nights Jonah waited, pleading with God, until the giant fish spat him back out.

***

He sat in the heart of the earth. It was dark, but he was light. It was warm and smelled of earth. And he was alive. He was one with the giver of life and had obeyed his every word. He had no regrets but was filled with relief and joy. Humanity was safe now because of his sacrifice.

Inside the heart of the earth, exactly as they had planned. For three days and three nights, Jesus remained until it was complete. Death could not hold him.

*One day some teachers of religious law and Pharisees came to Jesus and said, 'Teacher, we want you to show us a miraculous sign to prove your authority.'*

*But Jesus replied, 'Only an evil, adulterous generation would demand a miraculous sign; but the only sign I will* give them is the sign of the prophet Jonah. For as Jonah was in the belly of the great fish for three days and three nights, so will the Son of Man be in the heart of the earth for three days and three nights.' (Matthew 12:38–40)

# Hunger

Andrew had always been worried about food. He worried about where his next meal would come from and about whether there would be enough food for him. He worried about having to go without and trying to get to sleep on an empty stomach. The constant worrying made him feel stingy, and he wondered about why he was always so worried and about why he had an eye on the food allocations at all times.

It worried him that he didn't like to share. It made him feel as though he was greedy, so he tried to hide the way he felt. Nobody knew about his secret concerns. Andrew had watched those around him over the years, trying to pick up on clues as to whether he was alone, or whether others might be worrying about the food too. Was anybody else concerned that there would not be enough? Or that they might miss out?

But he had concluded he was alone in this. Andrew had gone to sleep hungry many times as a child and wondered if perhaps that had something to do with why he struggled now.

Today, Andrew was very hungry. He and the other disciples had been with Jesus on a hilltop beside the Sea of Galilee for many days now. Andrew knew exactly how much food they had left, and it wasn't much. By now, Andrew was so hungry that his hands trembled a little. Frustration was taking hold. And, to top it off, there were people everywhere! Andrew worried about how long it would be before he could finally eat.

'I feel sorry for these people.' Jesus pulled the disciples aside to speak to them. 'They have been with us for days now, and they have run out of food. I don't want to send them home hungry, or they will faint while they travel.'

Andrew's stomach grumbled. It was admirable how Jesus was always so concerned about everyone else, whereas Andrew's thoughts were consumed with his own hunger. He felt guilty as he listened to Jesus now.

'We could never get enough food for such a large crowd out here in the wilderness,' Peter exclaimed.

'How much bread do we have left?' Jesus asked them.

Andrew felt the skin prickle up and down the back of his neck. They didn't have enough for themselves, never mind having enough to think about sharing with this huge crowd. Andrew knew exactly how much food they had left.

'We only have seven loaves and just a few little fish,' Andrew replied. He tried to keep the concern from his voice.

'Sit down,' Jesus called out to the crowds of people. He turned from the disciples and directed the people where to sit. Jesus took the food from Andrew's trembling hands.

Andrew's blood sugar was low now. His heart sank as he watched his last meal walk away. Jesus thanked God for the food, then shared it out among the disciples to give out to the people.

Such a small amount of food wasn't going to go far. One thing was certain, Andrew wouldn't get to eat any of it. Andrew took some of the bread from Jesus and salivated at the thought of biting into it himself, as he handed it out to a family who sat nearby. It took all Andrew's remaining strength to try to keep his true feelings from showing on his face.

Andrew went back for more bread from Jesus and handed

it out to a group seated a little farther out. The bread would run out soon. But, as Andrew returned again and again and again, Jesus handed him pieces of the loaves again and again and again.

Finally, Andrew stopped before Jesus and looked from the seemingly never-ending loaf in his hand up into Jesus's eyes. What was going on here? Andrew had already handed out more bread than they had started with, and the other disciples were also sharing the loaves throughout the crowd. This made no sense. Jesus looked Andrew in the eyes, eyes full of knowing and full of love for Andrew.

'This piece is for you.' Jesus handed Andrew a large chunk of bread. 'Eat it,' he told Andrew as he placed it in his hands.

Andrew was so hungry, he did not hesitate but took a huge bite from the chunk of bread. He grinned at Jesus with his mouth full and took more bread in his free hand to share out with the crowd. Andrew should have known better than to doubt him.

*So Jesus told all the people to sit down on the ground. Then he took the seven loaves and the fish, thanked God for them, and broke them into pieces. He gave them to the disciples, who distributed the food to the crowd. They all ate as much as they wanted. Afterward, the disciples picked up seven large baskets of leftover food.* (Matthew 15:35–37)

# Revealed Identity

'How will I know which one you have chosen for me to build my church on?' Jesus asked.

'I will reveal to him who you really are,' God replied. 'Then you will know he is the one I have chosen.'

*Then he asked them, 'But who do you say I am?'*

*Simon Peter answered, 'You are the Messiah, the Son of the living God.'*

*Jesus replied, 'You are blessed, Simon son of John, because my Father in heaven has revealed this to you. You did not learn this from any human being. Now I say to you that you are Peter (which means rock), and upon this rock I will build my church, and all the powers of hell will not conquer it.' (Matthew 16:15–18)*

# Autumn

Autumn had never owned less in her life, but she had never felt the richness of joy overflowing like it was now either. What had happened in Autumn's life was miraculous, plain and simple, and Autumn was finding it hard to wrap words around—which was unusual, because Autumn was a writer.

She crumpled the paper on her tabletop. It was her second attempt to write home to try to explain to her parents why she was still here and what had taken place in her heart. To try to put into words just how powerful his name was. To try and explain that just last week, Autumn had watched a woman who was lame from birth stand up and walk around the room.

But it seemed useless. There were no words.

Autumn knew her parents would be uninterested. They hadn't had time for Autumn when she was a child, and she had felt unwanted and unloved. The rejection had followed her throughout her life. Even now, as a young woman, she could feel it buried within her. To be rejected by those who ought to love you best was not easily rectified. But Autumn would write to them anyway.

When she could find the words.

Just in case they wanted to come. To see for themselves.

Autumn felt at home here in a way she had never felt at home. Though her new friends had been strangers only a month ago, they now felt more like family, sharing all their possessions and all their money.

There was a sense of unity and community that was out of this world.

There was something that happened to Autumn when they met together and worshipped him ... it was as though everything that had ever mattered before—all the pain, all the rejection, all her heartache—was simply swept away. There was only Jesus. The joy was palpable and left her wanting more and more of him.

Which was why Autumn could not leave.

The people had formed a community. Every day there were new faces, their numbers growing and growing. Autumn was surrounded by like-minded people.

Someone walked by her tent. She recognised their voices—it was Hola and Shelo.

'Autumn.' Shelo sang out her name as they passed her tent door.

'I'm in here,' Autumn called back. 'I'll meet you there.' She smiled to herself. She was loved here, and—it seemed—she was wanted.

Autumn left her writing undone and ran her fingers through her hair. She grabbed another layer before ducking down through her tent entrance and stepping out into the last of the evening's sunshine.

They would eat together now, and she loved it all—the mealtimes, the jokes around the fireplace, remembering him with the wine and the bread, and most of all, the worship. When they joined as a community to sing out their praises to him, Autumn wondered if she would ever leave this place.

She had found the very meaning of life here, the meaning of her existence. Awe and wonder were her daily companions. Where else would she go?

*All the believers devoted themselves to the apostles' teaching, and to fellowship, and to sharing in meals (including the Lord's Supper), and to prayer.*

*A deep sense of awe came over them all, and the apostles performed many miraculous signs and wonders. And all the believers met together in one place and shared everything they had. They sold their property and possessions and shared the money with those in need. They worshiped together at the Temple each day, met in homes for the Lord's Supper, and shared their meals with great joy and generosity—all the while praising God and enjoying the goodwill of all the people. And each day the Lord added to their fellowship those who were being saved. (Acts 2:42–47)*

Let me see, so that I could turn to you, so that you
could heal me.

217

For the hearts of these people are hardened, and their ears
cannot hear, and they have closed their eyes—so their eyes
cannot see, and their ears cannot hear, and their hearts
cannot understand, and they cannot turn to me and let
me heal them. (Matthew 13:15)

# Birdie

The angels were talking about the little bird when the creator walked in. He looked at them with curious eyes.

'We saw a little bird on the mountains this morning,' an angel told him. 'She was so independent and delightful, busy flitting this way and that, playing all on her own, without a care in the world.'

'We all stopped to watch her,' another angel added.

God smiled. 'I know the one,' he said.

*For all the animals of the forest are mine,*
*and I own the cattle on a thousand hills.*
*I know every bird on the mountains,*
*and all the animals of the fields are mine.*
(Psalm 50:10–11)

# Hot House

He was light, and everywhere he stepped, there was light. He opened the front door to Satan's home and stepped inside. It was dark inside, but he brought light. He was not afraid, because he was God's Son.

The walls of Satan's home were red, and the stench of evil hung thick in the air. The temperature inside was too hot, but he was not deterred. He stepped through the living room and into the kitchen. He knew Satan was home. He spotted him now.

Satan sat at his dining table, where black candles dripped their wax straight onto the tabletop. Satan did not look alarmed when he saw him, but slowly rose from his chair to face him. Satan was very strong. You only had to look at him to see how strong he was. God's son looked Satan in the eyes for just a moment.

'Sit,' He commanded.

Satan's eyes burned like fire, but he was unable to protest. He sat back down.

God's Son fetched some rope from beneath the kitchen sink and used it to tie Satan to his own chair. Steam poured from Satan's ears. He was furious but was defenceless against God's Son. When Satan was secured and unable to break free, God's Son reclaimed the things in Satan's home. God's Son took the souls Satan had claimed as his own. God's Son took them and set them free.

God's son plundered the home of Satan while Satan sat and watched.

While Satan watched from his chair with his hands tied behind his back.

*But if I am casting out demons by the Spirit of God, then the Kingdom of God has arrived among you. For who is powerful enough to enter the house of a strong man and plunder his goods? Only someone even stronger—someone who could tie him up and then plunder his house.* (Matthew 12:28–29)

# The Valley of Weeping

Selby lived in the valley of weeping, and it was such a sad place to live. She hadn't meant to set up camp here, but grief had led her to the valley and now she didn't know how to leave. Everywhere she looked, whether to her left or to her right, there were tears.

The valley was flooded with tears, day in and day out. If the tears were not her own, they came from her neighbours. The sound of weeping drowned out any other noise, and the tears were neverending. They went on and on.

Selby hated living here. The valley of weeping broke her heart. She had never known such deep pain could exist until she had moved to the valley. It was a dark hole that consumed her, and she was sure she would never be free of it. Selby would live here forever.

All she could do was cling to him. All she could do was wait for him. Though she couldn't see him any more, and she could no longer feel him near, she sensed that the valley was blurring her vision. Had he been close by all along?

As the days became weeks and the weeks became months and the darkness of the valley held Selby captive, slowly but surely something began to shift. It was something about the tears. The tears that had been cruel and careless, stinging Selby's eyes. Had the tears softened somehow? They still flowed both day and night, filling up the valley all around her, but they no longer seemed to hurt Selby as they once had.

The tears filled the valley, but they were more like refreshing springs. The waters that had hurt her now seemed to help her, but how? Had he touched her tears? Come into her valley? Turned her tears to springs of joy?

The sun shone inside Selby's valley of weeping for the first time in a long time and she realised why. She realised that she could see him now.

*What joy for those whose strength comes from the Lord, who have set their minds on a pilgrimage to Jerusalem. When they walk through the Valley of Weeping, it will become a place of refreshing springs. The autumn rains will clothe it with blessings. They will continue to grow stronger, and each of them will appear before God in Jerusalem. (Psalm 84:5–7)*

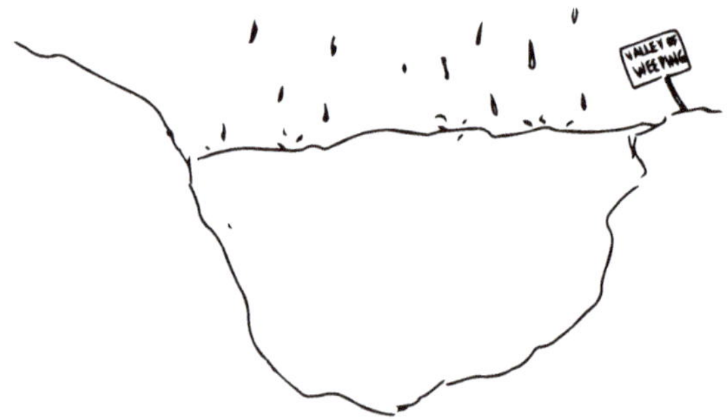

# A Story by Stacey

We were on holiday, and our young son was overtired from travelling. He was losing the plot, becoming more and more worked up and upset by the minute. We were beside the hotel pool, and I was trying to calm him down, but nothing was working.

Eventually, I held him down and lay him on a lounger. I began to massage his hands. He slowly calmed down as I moved up his arms and massaged his shoulders, his head, and his back. I ended up giving him a full body massage for almost an hour until he was so relaxed, I thought he might have been asleep.

I kissed his nose and whispered, 'I love you.' Then I left him to rest.

I joined my husband, who was ordering a drink at the poolside bar. My husband chatted with the bartender as we waited for our drinks and I worried about how anxious I was feeling. Here I was, on a much-anticipated holiday with my family. We were on a rooftop ordering a drink beside a pool … life didn't get much better than this!

But inside, I was full of anxiety and couldn't seem to shake it. I spoke to God as I stood beside the bar. I told him I felt anxious and far away from him. I asked if he could say one thing to me now, one thing to calm me down, if he could break through and meet me right where I was at, then what would he say to me?

In an instant, he showed me the way I had just laid my own child down on the lounger beside the pool. The way I had massaged his little hands, the way I had slowly moved up his arms to his shoulders, eventually massaged his entire body from his head down to his toes. How I'd kissed the tip of his nose and whispered that I loved him.

And I remembered I am God's child. That he loves me in that way.

In that instant, he reminded me how kind he is and how close he is, even when I feel far away. That instead of words, God would come near. He would treat me with such intimate, tender love and care, the way I did for my own child.

And I remembered again that this is the way he loves us.

Thank you for reading my stories through to the end. I hope you heard him whisper to you through the lines and the pages, and I hope you remembered that he sees you and knows your story.

That he listens to your words as you string together sentences and he watches your life with love-shaped eyes.

That when the cross weighed him down and he struggled to keep moving, he took another step because he thought of you.

He thought of your family, of your bloodline, of that beautiful familiarity you get when you step into your home and close the door to the world behind you.

Of your life.

He thought of you.

– Stacey

www.ingramcontent.com/pod-product-compliance
Lightning Source LLC
Chambersburg PA
CBHW061120100726
47911CB00013B/618